BOOK 4

Rise Of The Tenebris Times

FREDERICK ALEXANDER

PAGE PUBLISHING
Conneaut Lake, PA

First originally published by Page Publishing 2024

ISBN 979-8-89157-102-0 (pbk)
ISBN 979-8-89157-113-6 (digital)

Printed in the United States of America

CHAPTER 1

Hunter Talks to His Dead Father

FATHERS LOVE THEIR SONS, YES? BUT TO what extent would a father let his son become the same man he was, were his ways dishonorable, hatred-driven, a lustful heart, and an infested mind craving for power. Or will he become a good man?

In this tale, that is not the agenda of Zepa. He has marvelous plans for his kin to continue something ghastly. Even through death, he has his clever ways to interact, and Dacus shall guide his son on that journey of endless horror and death. After all, you've endured as well with our heroes who venture deeper into the planet. Knowing how the last tyrant succumbed to his own sins, can you recall who was still lying there in the darkness watching everything play out who knew that the greed of man and the wars they've fought fed his armies' souls, giving them strength soon able to leave their dark dimension? Raka is coming soon. But before this time, another being rules; by now you should surely know. Careful…do not say his name too loud; you don't know who might be listening. His followers are everywhere. His empire will finally become known to more.

Do you now see that Lord Montorious is the rightful ruler of this planet, or do you too still need convincing, believing in hope that will not come to the worms of Vospheron? Do not have pity for them for the mighty must always prevail over the weak. If you wish to save your heart from being torn in two, I would set this book down now before you go further into this world where even darker things than before will be unleashed…but take heart. After all, doesn't good always prevail?

*****

"Come, we are almost there. Watch your step!" Dacus gave Hunter a serious look. The two were walking through a weird marshland that was very eerie. Thick fog enfumed the air that blinded them in some areas, which made Hunter stumble into a huge equator of mud. "I-I'm sorry, master." Hunter's eyes grew big as he was still in the mud that actually was a home for some kind of monster that was trying to coil its odd-looking ligaments around the boy, but Dacus used his power to singe its body. This made the creature scream, uncoiling itself from the boy and retreating back into its home beneath the sludge.

"Quiet, youngling. Something more beastly than before is here with us. Do you not sense it?"

Hunter stood back up to his feet, trembling, trying to grasp the pale man's arm.

"Be strong, Hunter. It is coming…now." Dacus then disappeared, leaving the boy to fend for himself.

Hunter begun to hear a loud terrifying roar, briefly looking down a moment to see an immense shadow begin to cover the ground around him and above as he heard something fly over him. He breathed heavily, turning his head from the left to the right. A chill ran down his back while he began to create an odd mixture of matter in his hands. That lasted for a few seconds, then was gone as he quickly rushed to a nearby tree and hid behind it, his heart beating fast, too terrified to move, worried that whatever was coming would sniff him out.

As he stood there, he began to hear other frightening things in the vast forest of wildlife. Things howled and made noises that'd make simple-minded men go mad. There was a sudden loud roar that shook the ground. Hunter peeped his head out slightly and looked to the sky that was a purple color to see a huge giant flying creature. "A dragon!? It can't be… Those went extinct long ago! How am I supposed to best such a thing?" he asked himself aloud as he glanced down at his hands. Powerful light began radiating from them. He closed his eyes and took a deep breath, then exhaled and stepped back out into the marshland. His feet stepped in puddles of muck as huge equators had steam coming from them that brought revolting smells.

He looked above once more to see that the beast was on a rampage. Fires were seen in the distance. But wait…it was coming back!

Hunter quickly tried to manifest the same power before managing to do so, but it was too much, and he shot it out uncontrollably as it hit a large boulder far away, splitting it in two. The light continued to project out berserkly everywhere. It made him lose his balance and fall on his back. A loud snarl was heard suddenly from the enormous silver-skinned monster with an intricate orange design on its body bearing eyes that shone white. It had spotted him!

Folding its wings in, it swooped down fast with its giant mouth open wide, ready to swallow the boy whole!

Hunter grew frantic and quickly stood back up to leave this death trap, but unfortunately, the mud had made one of his feet become stuck. Hunter knew he had to act fast in building his power back up, or this place would become his tomb. Closing his eyes, waiting for the right timing, raising his hands to the skies, now he let out immense power that shot out from his hands and into the beast's mouth, lighting up the giant lizard's insides as its belly expanded and then imploded as chunks of its body flew everywhere, and some of his insides and other gross liquids fell on him and in his mouth.

The head fell right near Hunter's feet, and hot steam poured out of the bodiless cretin's mouth, rising in the air. Its big eyes stared back at him, widened. He looked back in horror at the creature, then looked down at his hands. "Did I do this?" he murmured aloud. He then turned his head away from the creature and threw up.

"Well done, well done."

The boy lifted his head from left to right to see if anyone was around, but no one was in sight. He wiped his mouth. "Dacus! Is that you? You can come out now. I beat your little game!" said Hunter, grinning with pride. Still there was no answer as the wind picked up all of a sudden, and the air became cooler.

"You still have a long way to go to unleash your true power, and only then will you have completed your full training to the dark side." This time the voice came from behind him as he spun around, only to get a glimpse of something sinister before it vanished once more. He'd seen a big creepy hand that had long black claws, and Hunter became frantic.

"Am I in hell for my father's past ways? Have I been cursed?"

"No, you're in a land far worse." The unknown being finally revealed itself right in front of him. He was slightly transparent, then randomly changed to having a more intact body with skin partly showing and bones showing all over his body and parts of his neck and face. His eyes looked like a blood river. "I am Raka. I will help teach you new powers, adding to what superb energy I already sense in you."

A loud noise was then heard. Dacus had returned and was standing next to the boy. In his wake where he stood was turquoise smoke mixed with energy. He laid a hand on the boy's shoulder. "Yes, we both will," he said, looking at the beastly man and giving him a slight grin, then nodded his head to him in respect.

At that moment, other men in black clothing with fancy weaponry and battle masks stepped out of the shadows of this mystic world and joined them.

"These are notable warriors from different sectors on Vospheron and different planets who will aid you on your missions as well when the time comes," said Dacus.

Why, you ask? What horrible plans did these powerful beings need him for?

His master, along with the rest, began to teach him many things, putting him through vigorous training fighting monsters in this strange place. Hunter learned to manifest dark magic, teleport, studied the hidden secrets on how to become immortal, and of course, how to raise his elemental powers to higher lengths. Ah, we must look at Hunter's example for just a little yeast makes the dough rise (as in Galatians 5:9). Little things he's exposed himself to have made him learn sinister things that are unholy, as in 2 Timothy 3:13. So we too must stay away from such things that we know to be wrong, such as tarot readings, crystals that you believe to have healing properties, Ouija boards. I speak to my brothers and sisters in Christ who have chosen to follow the Lord all powerful, do not forget I speak with love (1 Corinthians 5:12–13, 1 Peter 1:15–17, and Ephesians 2:10).

"He still isn't unleashing his true power. Maybe the fight with Akachi wasn't enough for him to awaken it?" said Raka, who turned his head toward Dacus, awaiting his reply as he watched Hunter spar with the six men who used martial arts skills and each of their unique powers that surged different colors.

"Yes, I don't know. I sense great conflict within his spirit. His accursed uncle's blood does run through his veins. I believe the good in him is trying to come out. We must eradicate whatever small light of good that still is trying to come out as we both know if your roots grow deep, nothing can stop the darkness from prevailing said Dacus. Dacus was right according to John 15:5–7."

"Agreed," said Raka.

At that moment, Hunter yelled as immense energy radiated from him, destroying trees, rocks, and little critters crawling across the ground as he threw the men into the air and then falling on the ground twenty feet from him. There was debris everywhere and high winds.

As he approached his two teachers, he was unable to harm them; there was some sort of force field around them that Dacus had created.

"Very good," said Dacus, smiling. "Your father would be proud."

Hunter grinned as he sweated immensely, breathing heavily, finally catching his breath. "Thank you, master. I believe I'm ready now for the next mission that Lord Montorious has for me."

At that moment, a huge creature roared and swept down next to the boy and nudged his face. He laughed as he patted its head for this was a jet-black lion that had massive wings and eyes that shone.

"Don't be hasty, Hunter. You barely got out alive when you went to Seluntacka. You must be patient. There is much more for you to learn and new challenges ahead at the next place," said Dacus.

Hunter sighed. "I just want to get back my other friends already. I can feel they're still alive. Barabus knows it too!"

The creature then roared mightily as his large tail swung back and forth.

"His brothers are family." Hunter looked at his teacher with slight sadness in his eyes.

"Control your emotions. Your enemies won't have any pity on you," said Raka. "Come, I have a test for you."

Hunter followed, pondering what could be worse than facing a dragon that he'd defeated so easily, beginning to become overconfident in his mind, plotting what strategy to use next.

They came to an enormous pit with red smoke that rose from it. "What is this?" asked Hunter.

Raka didn't say a word to him, only raised his hands in the air and began to speak in a different language. The air became colder, and the sky changed color to what almost resembled the northern lights. Rain started to fall down hard as Raka began to talk louder in this ancient language. As the last words were spoken, thunder rumbled, and lightning struck the sky.

Someone was arising out of the pit.

Hunter squinted his eyes to get a better look. The rain made it hard to make out who it was. The mysterious person floated from the pit and landed on the mushy marshland barefoot. The skies ceased its anger just as the sea does after a storm, but the sky was still eerie.

It began to move in a way that wasn't normal. "HUNTER!" said the ghoul in a deep voice as light rain began to fall.

What Hunter saw next made him take a few steps back. "It… it can't be."

Dacus then appeared instantly behind the boy and grabbed him by the arms as the same color shroud of smoke dissipated from him. "It's all right, don't be afraid," said Dacus.

Hunter then gazed upon what used to be a man. His eyes were a creepy color, body badly cut, his hair stained with blood as his neck had a deep cut where a sword had made its claim.

"Father." He began to tear up, falling to his knees. "I can't see you like this. It pains me so."

"You must look, son… Look at me. See what my own brothers did to me." Zepa balled his hands into fists in anger. "You must finish what I could not. Kill your uncles—it is the only way there can be true peace. Show them no mercy for they did not grace me with any."

Hunter began to cry. "Yes, yes, Father I will… I will!" he shouted. His eyes changed to pitch-black. "They shall pay for this unforgiving act. I will have my revenge!" Purple flames began to cover his body. He then walked closer to his father, then turned to look at his two teachers, grinning wide as the rest of the mysterious men he sparred with gathered, and his pet lion creature came up beside him and roared ferociously, sprouting out its majestic wings.

So it has begun…my word. The world will run red when the dark apprentice comes forth.

CHAPTER 2

Sacrifice

ONCE THE WAR BEGAN, SCAR FOUGHT VALIANTLY with his small brigade army and with Taguna's aid, but surely only two hours in, they were overwhelmed. Even the legions of winged beasts to Scar's aid were not enough to prevail over Montorious's overwhelming armies this time. They were so many new monsters of all sinister shapes and sizes.

Scar gave the signal to retreat as the few that were still alive tried to fight their way back to the ships as millions of men and those with powers were still waiting to fight as they stood near their rulers, each army bearing uniquely designed armor colors. Some that were elite troops bore drapes of red, yellow, and other shades of colors with battle masks. Others wore helmets that had enhanced tech on the screen to show them things about what was around their surroundings as other men and women wore fancy suits that deployed heinous destructive devices from their persons. Some used jet packs to attack Mandare in the air.

"What a beautiful sight, no? Look at them, frightened and outmatched. What a pitiful resistance," said Montorious as his eyes shone, gazing left to right upon everyone who was fighting still to let the rest escape.

My, my. Have you now chosen which side to follow? Will you die like the pawns of this story, or will you live and gain riches and glory with the master of this planet? I must admit, it angers even me that he's endured for this long, prospering while others are in pain.

But let it not make us stray from what we know is right and become so angry that we too want to do unholy things like the evil people of Vospheron and the damned beasts, for their time is almost at its end, as in Psalm 37:7–8. So let us carry on and see once more what awaits our heroes this time.

Montorious then spotted an old friend. "Ah, Scar, leaving so soon? We must finish what we started! Finish them off before they can escape!" he shouted.

"Yes, my liege," said a terrifying creature dripping drool onto the ground. He had blood orange fur with dozens of eyes, fangs like a spider, and four arms sticking out of his back, but had two legs. His arms were covered in fur as well as his feet. He had pointy ears that were a cream white color with red talons. He hissed to another creature just like him, but was multicolored. They spoke in different languages as the others raised an enormous flag bearing the insignia of their notorious master.

Hundreds of reptilian creatures took to the skies along with other ghastly beasts.

Scar rushed to pull out his device. Floyd was upon his shoulder; his beak and talons were stained in blood. Scar pressed a few buttons as the ramp extended out from his ship, and giant doors above the roof opened up as giant guns dropped down that were connected to machinery began shooting at the beasts and incoming contacts while some others were manned by robots.

Other huge bombs were shot at the enemy armies, but hundreds of mystic men created a force field protecting them as others perished in mass numbers.

"Someone take out those guns!" shouted an elite man higher in command as he stood with prestige with a spear that was half a sword and was gold, barking orders at other men in their combat armor. Dozens of men flew in the air with their jet packs, dodging many objects, trying to reach the ship but failed. Others flew in other medium-sized vehicles and shot their way through, but were picked off by Scar's forces as the rest from each army marched first in formation, shaking the ground, it seemed, as their drapes blew in the wind.

Montorious did not let any more of his army go forth. He wanted to see what his new subjects could do.

Scar was the first to get on board as hundreds of his robots stormed past him and charged at the enemy, letting the forces of good reach safe harbor. Taguna's forces bombarded, charging through full platoons by themselves, but these new enhanced men and their sorcery tech enhancements gave them an advantage. They could blame that bastard Xsuss for this; his cunningness had no end, even in death. Why have such evil forces come together from different parts of this planet to smite what last good is here? Maybe they should just give up and let them have Vospheron; surely they will not follow them elsewhere.

"Hurry!" Scar waved his hands in the air, helping people in while his other allies were getting on their vessels. Kanos and the others were still fighting their way to safety, slicing the heads off creepy damnations. Twelve to one every step of the way, Taguna saw from above that they weren't going to make it unless a sacrifice was made. Kanos and his kin began to create a major storm while they fought. Their eyes turned a mystic dark blue as thousands of giant ice spears fell from the sky, blocking off the enemy from them, creating a perimeter. Now there was a chance to make haste toward the ship.

All of a sudden, the three heard such an unsettling odd noise. They looked up at the sky while running as dozens of horned beasts with long tails and eyes that could look into your soul swooped down, blowing out flames of amaranth from their mouths. Many soldiers were running behind the elemental trio as well, but the flames changed into giant hands and grasped the soldiers, yanking them into the air, turning their flesh into skeletons. Bones and armor rained down from the skies.

"Well done, Rulugof," said one of the kings who had an interesting being that stood in front of him and their superb supreme leader.

The mysterious man had his hands raised, aimed toward the beasts, as if he had aided in amplifying their powers from afar with such precision. He lowered his hands, giving a slight grin beneath his face armor. Then he turned to face his masters and nodded his head.

Montorious rubbed his chin while still upon his new favorite pet. "Marvelous, yes. You shall be of great use to me. Is all of your kind back home this gifted?" he asked.

"I am the best," Rulugof stated. "Lord Montorious, there are more wondrous things back where I come from."

"There are many other unique individuals like him," said a king to his left.

"But don't forget, you too have your own wars to deal with. All of you in your own regions on this planet. These forces that we watch flee before us now, even more they harvest as we speak, like the grains of the sand enfuming elsewhere as other heroes are rising from the ashes," said Montorious.

"Yes, yes, we have had other beings from other districts and planets come here now to help in taking back the land for the people, but there is too much for them to fix to have the strength to muster to come here and help these rebels. No, no, we are evenly matched for now, I must admit. But you, my liege, here, you're doing the best."

Montorious rolled his eyes. "Oh, do stop. I was beginning to like you. Don't kiss ass now."

The man laughed. "Aye."

*****

"Whoa, did you see that!?" said Aaron.

"Just keep going, don't stop!" yelled Sabastain.

At that moment, fifteen men in jet packs flew overhead, shooting lasers from their guns at them, cutting them off ahead, but Kanos quickly electrocuted all of them. As their bodies lit up, a bright light shone on their visors as they yelled then dropped dead, bodies singed.

They rushed past burnt corpses, only to be stopped by eight winged beasts ahead, then ten more. They were surrounded and were the last survivors not aboard. All the other ships had already left except for Scar's.

"Let's leave them before we're all killed!" yelled a miserable whelp of a man who was on a gurney who'd lost a leg, and half his face on one side was scorched.

A nearby soldier slapped him across his face. "I outta throw you overboard, let Montorious's sea demons have you! How dare you speak such a thing after they risked their lives for you to make it back in one piece? Well, almost anyways. Hell, it'd been worse if they weren't on our side! Get him outta my sight!" he shouted as men rushed and hurried to treat his wounds.

"Stay strong, brothers," said Kanos.

Just when they thought it was the end, thousands of gargoyles came to their aid, slicing the heads of these giant abominations, showing them their might.

The three kin saw their effort and began fighting as well, but knew they weren't going to make it.

A giant gargoyle swooped down to Scar's ship. "Lord Taguna says to prevent further death, we must leave now. I suggest you do the same. Enough of our brothers and sisters have fallen today for man's wars once again," he said in a terrifying raspy voice, then sprouted its massive wings and shot back into the air and flew away from the battle along with millions more.

The engines of the ship steamed with smoke as Scar looked down in sadness for a moment, wishing he didn't have to do this as the ship's guns still bombarded the enemy's forces like Normandy. He took one last look at his friends who were still fighting for their lives.

Kanos had just formed an ice sphere to protect them. As he then looked at Scar, the ship pushed out, drifting away. Kanos nodded his head, giving him a serious look and a slight smile as he had blood and sweat mixed together running down his face. His hair stuck to his face. He knew now was the time.

All of a sudden, the same strange color as before engulfed the sphere, cloaking them from sight.

Scar then looked away in horror, almost falling to his knees aboard the deck, but caught himself, grasping the ships railing. His eyes raced back and forth, staring at the blood from wounded men that had flooded the top deck. "Is this real? I must be dreaming…

so much is lost… We've lost." Scar dared not look back for he knew what had become of his friends.

The ship was now a safe distance away, but of course, the enemy wouldn't be too far behind for they would soon spread their evil farther into this region for all would now know the might of Montorious. No one can stop this movement of a new world order rising.

Adam took command and set a course for a city he'd seen up ahead while first stopping by a local tavern outpost, a place where you can get a quick bite to eat and trade goods, while Scar tried to grasp the truth of what happened to his friends who took their toll.

They traveled farther into new uncharted waters of this world. What awaited them would soon be unveiled.

Scar lay in his bed, staring up at the ceiling, wondering if his enemy had conquered his world already. Were they all dead? Would Mr. Benson still be outside watering his plants on the back deck? Was Scar's favorite place to get his midnight cravings of ice cream still intact? That diner where he could get the best bacon cheeseburgers and Oreo cheesecake shake. So much had been taken from him, so why bother with anything? All his closest friends were almost gone. Only Pragticus, Obek, and Adam remained.

Scout lay on his master's body, resting his head on his chest as the ship reached port near a huge outpost farther in the mountain range that had houses and roads and many big buildings and such, but you could also rent out rooms in this tavern.

Scar's robots guarded the outside of the ship to protect them while Taguna's army stayed in the harbor scavenging for food in the water as some slept on top of the ship.

Adam left the ship to see if he could find any willing able-bodied men or women who would join their cause. He walked across the squeaky bridge that led over to the diner, and a few soldiers went with him to get a drink.

Once they were inside, there were many monsters and people laughing, having a great time. Some were watching a sport of some kind on a floating robotic screen; others were playing cards, betting on a fight between two species in a boxing ring; while farther away on a stage, pretty women danced and were singing a song. Others fought each other from being drunk.

Adam looked over at the bartender to see he had two heads and a cluster of eyes in the middle of each face and eight arms making many drinks at once. "Go unwind a bit, my comrades. On me!" said Adam.

The men cheered, rushing over to the bar while others went off to dance with women. While their leader took a seat at a table, a captivating woman came by and asked him what he would like. She later came back with brown rice and a plate filled with an assortment of meats and a pitcher of some fizzy blue drink that had orange swirls in it.

While he began to delight in this meal, someone was watching him from afar, smoking a cigar. He wore a hood over his head and overheard they were looking for men to join them. Some didn't care for they knew that Montorious didn't care about neutral parties such as them. They were scallywags themselves. Others had lost so much already and were too afraid; still, many wanted excitement.

The man held a long black staff in one hand.

Hours passed as hundreds to thousands of men came through the post and decided to join, but of course, they were not enough to even be a fraction strong enough to break through the forces of the many armies with their unforeseen tech in this region.

Adam was putting people in his tablet of summaries about them. The man walked over and placed his staff on his shoulder, leaning over a bit to look at the man he was analyzing. He then started to laugh. "You believe these simpleminded drunken fools are what can stand against you-know-who? You're gravely mistaken. What you need is real power. Crystals that can give your entrusted men the power to conquer your enemies," said the man, who began to grin as he began to smoke his cigar and puff out smoke into intricate shapes, awaiting a reply.

Adam didn't know what to say; his face had an expression of disbelief. "Where are these crystals you speak of, and if they hold what you say, why haven't you gone yourself?"

"Because, lad, the journey to retrieve them is unspeakable. The horrors that obstruct your opportunity to grasp them is paralysis." The man's face became stern, but he then smiled once more while grabbing Adam's pitcher and poured himself a glass. "Hmm, I would have to talk to my friend about this. Well, what're we waiting for? We aren't getting any younger!"

Adam nodded slightly, smirking. He then stood up and led the tall man to the ship once they were aboard Adam ordered a soldier to go to the tavern and round up any more men who'd like to come for they would be leaving soon.

The two then proceeded to Scar's quarters. Adam knocked on the door.

"Enter."

They did so to see Scar was practicing his combat skills, kicking a rubber body that was on a pole, then he threw dozens of punches after that and switched to a wooden structure that had poles sticking out that he used martial arts techniques on.

"Scar, I have someone you must meet." He told him what the interesting man spoke of before.

Scar just laughed as sweat rolled down his face while Floyd, at the moment, flew overhead and dropped a clean towel on his friend's head that he then used to wipe his face.

"I'm sorry, we still don't even know your name," said Adam, who turned to look at the stranger.

"My apologies." He then put his cigar out in his hand then reached over to shake Scar's hand. "Name's Ezra, and what I say is true. There are crystals out there that have powers. Don't you want another day of hope to rid this planet of its vile, sinister beings?"

Scar poured himself a glass of water while he then stared out the window of his room for a moment. He sighed deeply, then turned around. "Start the engines. We have some crystals to find." Scar smiled.

"Fantastic! Once we do find one, you have the privilege of using it on yourself," said Ezra.

"No, I don't think I'd want to, only if I hadn't another choice."

Ezra laughed. "Aye," he said.

"Come, one of my robots can show you to a room." Scar gestured one hand toward the door.

Robots were passing by outside the room as Scar opened the door and turned their gazes upon Ezra as they then proceeded down the hall with them.

"Here are the coordinates to where our new associate said we should go first." Adam was pointing at a piece of paper.

Scar looked down, examining it. "We've had great losses, but we shall prevail and do what we must to defeat this evil, to defeat…" He paused. "I'll go give this to the navigator."

As Scar walked away, Adam pondered what awaited them in the future, as did many. Where did Taguna's part play in this tale? For his war was over, would he now leave and find a new home or stay?

The more they ventured farther into this new domain, thousands more joined, but as hope seemed to be rising, dark forces were also making their next move.

"Rulugof!" shouted a man who was watching people be imprisoned in slave ships. "Ha, Akachi will be pleased with his newly acquired help, don't you think?"

"Yes, sire, you called?" said Rulugof.

"Yes, Lord Montorious wishes for all of Xsuss's old counterparts to have one man with exceptional traits to be fortified into an extremist team made to kill the remaining scum. Do you have anyone in mind?" he asked.

"Yes, and they will be ready to leave in a fortnight's time," Rulugof stated.

"Well, go on then," said his king.

The man nodded, then extended out his arm in the air and made his hand into a fist, then placed it on his chest, lowering his head. He then spun around, rushing to get things done. He walked for a while, then pushed open two massive doors. "Aris, Lero, Damaris, Cyrox, and Jaxer!" he shouted.

Five men then rushed and stood in a line, all bearing different-colored armor and gear, and a few had drapes that were different colored as well with insignias on their enhanced armor wearing battle masks.

"Make sure you're ready to leave soon. We'll have much ground to cover, and we cannot fail. Do you understand?" Rulugof asked.

"Yes, sir!" they all shouted.

"Sir, the Gurazin are almost here, but they ate some of our men when acquiring them," said Lero.

"Ah, the fools. They weren't meant to be one of us. Come, let us gather the rest of my squadrons," said Rulugof.

The men then rushed out as they walked down the hall and made a left. They walked some more, did another left then a right, and opened a door to a massive assembly area where flying vehicles were being enhanced and placed on massive ships. Men were shocking Gurazin with long weapons with immense power. A thousand men were already in formation as Rulugof's headmen rushed to join certain groups.

Rulugof smiled wide, nodding his head. "Hail the Daemon guard!" he shouted, raising his hand that was balled into a fist.

The rest then shouted back, repeating what he said, raising their hands into the air into fists as Rulugof then put on his black-and-silver helmet that hid his face. Another person stepped beside him who wore dark purple attire mixed with black. Her eyes were bright with heterochromia. She had long red hair and two guns on her hip.

"Avonna, what're you doing here? This is my operation." He gave her an unpleasant look.

"Oh, do stop now. You know you always love to see me." She gave him a captivating smile as she gently touched his battle mask armor. "Just wanted to say farewell and hope you find what you're looking for, though I wanted to share that glory with you," she said, glaring into his face screen helmet, then spun around as her hair blew in the air, strutting away with her curvy physique.

Rulugof turned to look as she walked away.

"Careful, brother, you know she only wants one thing," said a man who slapped his shoulder then laughed.

Rulugof shook his head. "Yeah, you'd know all about that," he stated.

"I'm just kidding, fam. I know you care for her despite her lust for riches," said the man in red armor, who wielded a staff in one hand that was gold and had two heinous swords on his back and other treacherous things upon his person.

The two watched as the Daemon guard men marched onto the ships strategically.

"I just wanted to say farewell and good hunting. We had a swift victory today, but I sense that they have more to put out than what was shown."

Rulugof looked at his brother for a moment. "Goodbye, Euu'nn-ralla. Hail the Daemon guard!" Rulugof said, raising his hand in the air then extended his arm out in a pose.

His brother then did the same. "Hail the Daemon guard."

The two then connected their heads together with their helmets and hugged briefly as Rulugof then flew into the air and landed in a battle pose while the last squadron was entering the ship. He entered and passed hundreds of Gurazin that were roaring ferociously as he pressed on and went to the upper deck as he saw the ocean ahead.

The ship shortly after began to move along with the rest, pressing through an enormous kingdom then out to the open sea.

Rulugof then took off his helmet and slightly grinned as he looked out afar to sea. "So, Scar, let's see what you're really made of."

CHAPTER 3

Ezra the Benevolent

Infinite power is marvelous, is it not? Giving you strength you've only dreamt of, you become notorious by many. Some may even be naive enough to worship you and call you a god! But then more powerful beings than them show them just how feeble they really were all along as they cower back into the darkness, angry and afraid, remembering who is really in charge. Just as Lucifer does when he hears the name of the Lord Almighty, he must flee in Jesus's name (James 4:7, KJV).

So what's the point? Why gain something so massive when someone is always right behind you, waiting their turn?

Ezra has given Adam hope these crystals can bring help. What wondrous secrets do they hold?

The treacherous journey for them has already begun, testing the heroes of this tale. Darker beasts than even Taguna himself will be lurking about. Will even he give up from all the many powerful beings claiming new ground?

While the ship continued on its course through uncharted territory, a fortnight had already passed. Scar was a lot better than before for his depression had ceased, though he'd never forget what his friends did for them. He left his room and made his way to the top deck, then proceeded to the back of the ship, resting his arms and leaning over the railing.

It was very foggy outside while Scar was lost in his thoughts. A giant figure suddenly appeared out of the eerie fog right in front of him. Scar's eyes enlarged slightly, but saw who it was and remained at ease.

The creature flapped his massive wings and landed beside him. It had a giant sea creature in its mouth that was still thrashing, though it was locked in his massive teeth. There was then a loud snap.

Scar looked up at the beast. "I don't know how you eat that raw." He looked away in disgust.

"I don't see why you bring humans on your voyage of justice who don't even know which way is up."

Scar gave Taguna a puzzled look. Taguna then slapped one of Scar's legs with his tail, then used it to point at something as Scar's face then turned red while rubbing his leg. He then looked over to what he was referring to. There was a sad excuse of a man lying on a bench with a huge belly and a scruffy beard talking to himself in his sleep, holding a bottle of liquor in one hand as he had a piece of half-eaten pastry in his other hand that was upon his chest.

Scar scratched his head. "I was not with Adam when he… acquired…er, um, yeah."

Taguna grunted as he grinned slightly, showing the scales that were stuck in between his teeth from his meal. A door was then suddenly swung open a few feet from where they stood.

Ezra stretched his arms out. "What a beautiful eerie day." He twirled his staff, walking down the deck in the opposite direction from Scar. Gargoyles soared over the ship, bursting through clouds.

Taguna watched Ezra from afar as his eyes glowed a low silver.

Scar looked at him. "What's wrong?"

"Are you really going to trust this man? You barely know him."

"I didn't know you, and look what happened," said Scar, smiling as Taguna grunted once more.

"We had common goals when we met."

"So what're you saying?" He looked at the beast, awaiting a reply.

"I will not lead my family to their deaths because of one human's hunger for power. We are no longer slaves to that demon Xsuss. I've known his kind for centuries."

"We will use some of the crystals we find to help our cause. We need this to defeat our new enemies as well as old ones. You've seen already how many new powers they've unleashed, new mystic men and women with strength to plunder. My old friends had great power, and I cannot simply rely on others to do what I can do if I have the resources to do it."

"You humans, always looking for an easy fix, turning to false gods for help. Can you not see surely this will be your destruction just as it was for Xsuss?"

The beast was right for great blessings belong to those who don't turn to demons and false gods for help, according to (Psalm 40:4 ERV) Just as many people in entertainment have done to gain their fame.

Taguna then sprouted his wings. "I shall now withdraw. If you need me, I shall come to your aid."

Scar quickly pulled out his device and pressed a button as a flash of light emerged, then a small circular chip was in his hand. "Here, take this. When I need you, it'll blink blue, and this insignia will pop up, showing you a hologram of it."

Scar and Taguna watched as it did so, and the beast then smiled. "Ah, so you've finally picked a mighty symbol. What's the name of your team?" he asked.

Scar looked down for a moment, then slightly smiled and looked back up. "I'll have to get back to you on that. I hope that you are a part of it once I do have the full team?"

The monster gave him a look, then slightly grinned and lifted his head to the skies and shot into the air, giving a mighty roar. His followers heard his voice as millions followed.

Scar was now only left with a few friends: Pragticus, Adam, and Obek.

Not many heroes are left to lift the veil of darkness on this planet Vospheron. While they try to make haste in search for this new presumable power, more nations submit to Montorious's rule, committing blasphemy by proclaiming him as a god.

But he isn't one.

The fools… They'll never learn.

Ezra gazed upon the water, breathing in the fresh air and exhaling. "This is too divine! I could get—"

Before he could finish his sentence, he felt a terrible pain as something struck his head. He groaned low, almost falling to the ground as he caught himself by using his staff as support as it began to glow a mystical color from the rock on top. The water began to make a whirlpool in front of him, and he suddenly heard a strange voice speak to him in his mind: *Where is it... Where is it?*

He finally pulled himself together as sweat trickled down his face. As he gazed upon the water, a grotesque face appeared.

"Why have you summoned me in such an ill manner, my lord?"

"Silence!" said the figure in the water as it then spoke in a different language, asking him more questions. He replied in the same language.

"You better hurry. I grow tired of your failures." The figure then disappeared, and the water returned back to its serene state.

Ezra looked to the ground of the ship his eyes raced back and forth. *I'm running out of time.*

Curse Ezra! Can no one new be trusted? Has everyone in the land been warped by the demons of this world? This is only a grain of sand of the many secrets that lie waiting to be revealed hidden behind locked doors with chains in the minds of unknown persons. As some will try to break free these secrets, they should leave well enough alone in affairs that aren't their concern.

Months passed by while crossing the sea. Adam trained the men aboard to be ready for a fight while Scar continued to improve his device that assisted him much. Some men grew restless. Those asinine pigs wanted action, but they would soon wish they hadn't. One man climbed up a ladder to a post lookout. "We've almost entered the reef of Yahguden, Scar!"

Ezra clenched his staff at the mention of its name.

"Good, we'll acquire what we're looking for soon," replied Scar.

"Don't be so sure. A foul darkness awaits us once we approach there," stated Ezra while many men laughed at him, calling him unsettling names.

"Our guide is such a schoolgirl!" one shouted.

"Make fun as you wish, but the story of that reef is true."

"Bah, that old wives' tale," another replied.

Scar's face seemed intrigued. "What is this folktale that has so many of you in disbelief? Are gargoyles not enough for it to be true?" said Scar.

"It's okay, Scar. I don't expect closed-minded worms such as these that have barely left the nest while their momma's stench from them leaving the womb is still on them with their umbilical cords tied around them like the brigands they are." Ezra gave a crooked grin at the men.

The group of men rushed over, about to toss him over, until Scar stepped in. "Enough! Tell me the story." His friends gathered in to hear as well.

"Very well. Long ago, gypsy women traveled the sea, healing those who needed help. They used their medicines and power for good, but of course, some saw this as devil work, perceiving them as witches, so pirates attacked them, made them watch them kill their husbands and children, then did horrible things to them, robbed them. Lastly, the same fate was their own gutting them like pigs, slicing their beautiful faces, afterward tossing their bodies into the ocean near the reef of Yahguden and burned their ship. The pirates laughed, satisfied in their deeds of 'good work' for the day. What they didn't know was that a crystal was at the bottom of the seabed that fed on their pain and hatred that consumed their souls in death, so it gave them life once more. Well, somewhat."

Ezra swallowed hard.

"It turned them into hideous creatures with red eyes, long scruffy hair, pale blue skin with long black claws, hot foul breath, and sharp teeth. They wore dirty, bloodstained dresses. They quickly got over how they looked and thanked the crystal for giving them the opportunity for revenge. The pirates, the evildoers they were, didn't leave the reef, no, only casted anchor and had a festival on their vessel. Suddenly, they began to hear loud terrifying moaning and groaning of something, then loud screeching. Their eardrums popped as blood oozed out. This killed a few of the older men by just that alone as others became death from burst ear drums only able to see the horrors unfold. They were the lucky ones unable to hear the screams and the ripping of flesh from their friends' bodies from them being devoured."

Ezra smirked, shaking his head.

"They swarmed over that ship so quickly, killing everyone aboard, leaving trails of blood everywhere, and torn insides of men lay in places. Skulls were open, hollowed out by some of those lovely ladies eating their brains and drinking the blood out of it. But now today, they're still there, awaiting for more men to stumble upon the reef to have their way with them. There's at least two dozen of them, so they say." At that moment, Ezra lit a cigar and began smoking it.

Scar was in deep thought for a moment, then rubbed his chin briefly. "You speak of that story with such emotion, as if you were there," said Scar.

Ezra just slightly smiled, nodding his head as he puffed out smoke, casually tapping his staff. "Oh yes, I almost forgot, the only things able to kill these beautiful ladies of the night is salt and gold weaponry."

Scar looked at Ezra for a moment. "I'll have to create protective gear for our ears, strong enough to withstand their screams and other intricate things." He then walked off to work quickly as they'd reach the reef sometime tomorrow.

The rest of the men who were walking about were told the story by comrades later, but then relaxed and continued on with their daily antics, not caring, eating, partying, and drinking with one another. Some even had relations with each other as well as with women. Scar wanted warriors; he did not care for their choice of living (as in Ecclesiastes 11:9–10 and Matthew 24:37–39).

Floyd watched his friend work while perched upon his head. "Hope this works, or I'll have to find another human to feed me well and steal food from," said Floyd, leaning down over Scar's head, trying to look his friend in the face, smiling as Scar rolled his eyes.

"Of course, you fatty. This will work. Now stop goofing around and let me focus. While the crew deals with the monsters, Adam, Pragticus, Obek, and I will go into the water and grab the crystal right from under their noses."

"Yeah, I don't think they have that anymore. As you humans say, slice and dice, is it?"

"Not funny, Floyd." Scar raised his head to look at his furry-faced, three-eyed companion, whose eyes were in the alignment of a triangle.

"I'm just saying." He fluttered his wings and puffed out his chest and began cleaning himself briefly. "So do you really want to risk using it on yourself? What if you become something worse than those creatures?"

Scar stopped working and set his equipment down. "No, it will not. My heart is good. It's not perfect, but I seek justice for all, for all of the evil ones who try to claim your world. I believe it'll grant me the pure power to do so." Scar then looked at his friend, who was giving him a serious expression.

"I'm with you, just afraid of the outcome."

Scar nodded his head. "Don't worry, if you happen to get affected by the crystal as well, I don't think it's possible for you to get any uglier than you are now," he teased.

Floyd nipped his ear. "So you think you're a comedian now?" said Floyd.

Scar chuckled as he then looked back down at his equipment. "Sacrifices must be made for the greater good." His hands began to tremble, remembering what his friends did as his mind raced back to the day, flooding him with horrible memories. He suddenly then pictured two giant hands trying to grasp his neck as a loud voice boomed, "DIE! DIE!" Two bright gold eyes appeared as the hands were now on his neck.

"Scar! Scar!" shouted Floyd as Scar managed to break free from the trance he was entrapped in. "Are you all right?" asked Floyd.

Scout came up licking his master's hand.

"I'm good." Scar then stood up and walked to a table in his room that had a pitcher on it filled with some form of liquid and poured himself a glass.

"Maybe you should rest, Scar. I'll wake you when we get close to—"

Scar cut him off. "No, by then it'll be too late." He walked back over to his desk. "I've finished the protective gear to withstand the creatures' scream. Go and give this to Adam, tell him to press this button to access them and the other accessories." He then picked up his ear gear that he was working on and put it in his then both his furry companions.

Once Adam received the device, he quickly did what Scar ordered as some were reluctant on putting them in. "Look here, if you value your lives, put them in," said Adam to four men who were kicking back, smoking cigars, drinking, and eating.

"We don't need that crap. There isn't anything out there. Go on now, boy!" shouted a built man.

Adam just shook his head, walking away. *Those arrogant sea rats! So be it, their pride shall be their demise.*

While Adam continued with making sure everyone got what they needed, men picked up what had the shape of some type of styled grenade that was filled with salt and also gold swords, spears, and archery from a variety of crates. While the air became colder, it stung the men's face. They could see their own breath when they spoke, as if they were having a smoke sesh.

As the water suddenly began to have bright colorful lights shine from the bottom, heavenly aromas filled the air. Many men gathered on both sides to gaze upon the exquisite colors, but what they didn't perceive was that they had entered the reef of Yahguden.

CHAPTER 4

The Wailing Women of Yahguden

Tʜᴇ ꜰᴏᴜʀ ᴍᴇɴ ᴡʜᴏ ᴡᴇʀᴇ ɪɴ ᴅɪsʙᴇʟɪᴇꜰ from before were all huddled together, looking at something that seemed to be emerging from the water. It was a gorgeous woman who had sparkling green eyes, pearl skin that glowed, and she wore a white gown. Her body was well put together.

The men became like hounds in for the kill, and she giggled a sweet laugh. "What are handsome men like you doing all the way out here? Come join me in the warm waters. It'll be worth it."

Three more women at that moment emerged from the water, all more beautiful than the last.

"See, now we're even." She smiled, raising her hands.

Without any hesitation, the four took off their shirts and jumped in and swam toward these enchanting ladies while more of their kind swarmed on either side of the ship. More men were about to take a dip until Obek stopped them. "What're you doing, you fools! Can't you see these are siren? That bastard Ezra did not tell us of this!" He tied a bandanna over his face so he could not breathe in the fumes that filled the air as he then slapped a soldier in his face. "Wake the hell up!"

The man then shook his head. "Oh, what happened?" he asked.

"Put this over your face, all of you!" shouted Adam, who passed out black bandannas.

"Archers, aim for their heads!" said Pragticus.

One of the women with the men in the water glanced up at the ship of what was about to happen, but she still smiled, caressing the man's face while she then placed her hand upon his waist with her other hand around his neck. She began to change in color. She bit her own lip so hard, blood appeared, running down her neck to her chest.

He watched, becoming so aroused. He leaned in for a kiss, closing his eyes. Once he opened them, he looked in horror for the pretty woman from before was no more. Instead, a hideous creature of the abyss was staring back at him. He was frozen in terror. It was too late. She then extended her long claws and dug them into the man's shoulders. You could hear bones cracking as she wedged them in deeper. He cried in agony, kicking his legs, trying to break free. Managing to muster some strength, he lifted his arm and socked her in the face, breaking her jaw. She growled low as she fixed her jaw using no hands, and there was a loud snap. She then hissed and lunged back her head as teeth grew out like giant needles. She lunged at his throat now, ripping out his esophagus. The rest of his group were also killed horribly as another drowned. I dare not speak of what else.

"Fire!" shouted Adam.

Dozens of arrows soared through the air, hitting the beasts. At that moment, loud wailing was heard from above as long dark-haired women swooped down and yanked men into the air. One unfortunate man had a horrid woman yank his head off as his lifeless corpse was still standing. Blood spurted out like a fountain as it wobbled over and fell off the side, slapping the water while other corpses from the upper decks rained down, men that were torn to pieces.

The women in the water swarmed over them like piranhas, devouring them. Some were still alive, screaming, trying to fight back. Banshees took care of what was above as they wailed loudly, but didn't see anyone falling victim to their notorious howls.

"*Sister* coven! Man has become creative in their magic. They shield themselves from your notorious howls, so we shall rip those magic trinkets from their ears!" One stood upon a massive rock that was covered in algae. She was barefoot, very attractive with glowing blue eyes, purple hair, and an exquisite body. She also had long claws on her hands and feet.

Oh, such beauty but deadly. These heartless women craved revenge from any man.

Many swooped down and saw that there were also a few women in their ranks helping fight. This made them wail even louder.

"Traitors!" one shouted.

"We'll hang you from the sails!" said another who had blue-tinted hair and peach-colored skin.

Was accepting a new life worth the outcome for these monstrous ladies if they still have no peace?

While she stood there, the siren sang an intricate tune that wasn't to lure men. No, it called something else to them.

Three enormous sea serpents that were different in color—dark red with black design all over its body, yellow, and turquoise—all raised their bodies out of the water. One siren spoke to them in a different language as they all made a terrifying noise and attacked different levels of the ship, crashing through walls to attack their prey.

"These men have built a fortress that floats, but we will claim every last one of them," said the woman upon the rock.

The siren began to use their claws to climb up the ship as men shot arrows at them to knock them back down.

"No, you imbeciles! Use the other arrows. The gold ones are for the other foul beasts!" said Obek as a banshee tried to attack him, but he cut her in the chest. She yelled and cursed as another then swooped down near him and fought to get the sword from him. "Let go, you bitch!"

She laughed. "Now that's no way to talk to a lady." She then roared, trying to bite him as the other from before came running on all fours toward them.

Obek quickly reached for a grenade and finally managed to push the other woman beast off him. As he pulled the stick, he waited briefly and threw the grenade. It then exploded right when they were upon him. They screamed in agony as their skin burned, and they shriveled up as he was flung into the air upon one of the sea serpents.

"Oh great," he said as he tried to hang on so he wouldn't be flung into the ocean and become the buffet special for the day.

Adam fought back to back with Pragticus.

"Damn! Where's Scar?" said a soldier as a banshee tried to come from above and grab Adam, but he was too spry and sliced off her arms. Green mist sprayed out as she screeched, but then began to laugh evilly. Her nubs began to reform again, creating ligaments. She then blew him a kiss and said, "Next time, baby."

Pragticus spat on the ground and shouted not-so-nice words at her. "How do we expect to defeat these things? The crystal must be enhancing these strange cretins' powers. We must find it, but with that legion of sea devils in the water, it is impossible. We must make haste!"

Scar took Floyd's advice and took a nap, but slept too long since he had made his protective gear to also work as headphones so he could listen to music. He awoke and cut off the music on the side button on his equipment to hear the sound of hell raging on his ship. He looked outside the window, peeking out from the curtain a little. His eyes grew big as he rushed to get dressed.

"Floyd, you bum! You didn't wake me. Floyd!?"

The fat bird was snoring and had a pile of sweets that he used as a pillow.

Scar was now fully dressed and ready to leave when he heard a loud pounding at the door. This awoke Floyd, and Scout barked and growled immensely and ran around all frantic.

"Scar, there's someone—" Before he could finish his sentence, his friend gave him a scowl. Floyd scratched his head with his wing. "I lost track of time."

There was then another loud pounding on the door.

Scar slowly crept to the door while having one hand on his weapon, then opened the door. It was a man covered in blood, clothes dripping wet with deep cuts all over his body. "Scar! Do you have any more of that stuff for your ears? I need it please! I...I... ahhh!" shouted the man, covering his ears in horror. "She's back!

Bloody hell, kill me!" The man staggered away like he was drunk, then fell to his knees. He quickly reached for his gun and shot himself in the head.

Shortly after, Scar saw men running down the hallway for their lives. They were being chased by five banshees. "Quickly, in here!" Scar shouted, but the men were too slow as they were eaten. Then the carnivorous monsters saw their next target. Wailing, they soared toward the room.

Scar shut the door in a hurry as they slammed into it hard, cracking it, scratching claw marks deep through the metal door as he barricaded it quickly, but it wouldn't hold for long. He piled grenades filled with salt in a box and hid with his friends and waited.

"We're coming in! Let us suck the meat off your bones!" one shouted as they pushed through his measly defenses as they all were in a huddle.

"Get back, you wenches!"

They laughed. "Oh, you're handsome. We might have to keep this one, ladies. Have our way with him, make him our slave!"

Their eyes all shone even brighter now.

"Not today," said Scar as he raised his gun and shot the grenade bundle and ducked down, covering his friends.

There was a loud boom and horrifying groans, then the room was shrouded with green mist.

Floyd peeked his head out. "Phew, they reeked."

Scar stood up. "Let's go!" He rushed to the exit and hopped over the foiled fort.

"Ahem, yeah, I think it's best Scout and I stay here to, you know, tell the story of how the great Scar fought valiantly."

Scar slightly tilted his head and slightly grinned, then took off down the hallway that looked like bloody Mary. There was a monster in the corner feasting on a man's skull, slurping out all the nutrients she could, and then she lifted the corpse up at an angle so she could guzzle the sweet nectar.

"Hey, ugly, that's not very good table manners!" said Scar.

She raised her head and wailed as Scar threw a gold dagger at her head. At that moment, he heard someone yell for help. He rushed to the ledge to see Obek tussling with a big red serpent that he was stabbing with his sword. Scar laughed. "If this is a dream, God, let me wake up already!" He then jumped down onto the serpent and shot it in the head multiple times.

As it went tumbling over, Scar and Obek quickly jumped back onto the ship. It then crashed back into the sea as its other half hung from the ship, dangling. The two went to find Adam so Scar could retrieve his device to acquire diving gear to grab the crystal.

Once they made their way to him, Scar gave each of his friends what they needed as the four went down to the ocean floor.

The queen of the banshees and leader of the sirens saw them leave. "No matter, our other pet shall deal with them," said the banshee.

"Veronica, these men fight differently than past souls," said the siren.

"Do these mortal men scare you, Jezara? My company can finish them off." Veronica grinned wide as she twirled her hair, watching as men were still dying, but the siren next to her just rolled her eyes.

The four swam deep, passing by many aquatic life. Giant clams that had beautiful giant-sized colorful pearls were opening and closing their mouths incessantly. Those pearls would surely bring great riches, but finding the crystal was more important.

"Go away!" shouted a deep voice. "I can hear you coming in your wretched man technology. Leave now while you still can."

"Well, least we know we're close. Come on, guys. This way," said Scar.

The four continued swim a little farther till they saw something shine through a big crevice. As they approached closer and went through, a beautiful crystal was sitting in a pile with lots of other treasures and gold cups that had rubies designed around them. All of a sudden, a dark large shadow covered the seabed. Big creepy eyes appeared from this creature with long pink-and-red tentacles. It also had a giant beak. "You will not take what you seek. I won't let you," said the grotesque sea creature.

"Look out!" shouted Pragticus.

Everyone dodged just in time. They pulled out their weapons, stabbing into the thick slimy skin of this superb foe. It roared lividly, swatting them against rocks. The beast then spewed out some type of black ink from its body.

"I can't see!" shouted Adam, who swung his sword violently at nothing.

A loud laugh was heard. Tentacles were soon grasped around Scar and his friends tightly, making them unable to move, trapped in the grasp of their doom.

"Goodbye, heroes of the weak."

The beast then lunged out more tentacles that reached for their mouthpieces that supplied them with air while they squirmed to break free. It was useless until a green figure holding a gold weapon swam swiftly to them and sliced off the four tentacles that would have ended them. The mysterious thing kept slicing off limbs as odd-colored blood sprayed everywhere.

The beast tried to ink him but missed. The manlike creature used his weapon swiftly, like a fan. "Not this time!" stated the creature. He then pressed a button on his sword, which changed into a purple trident that he aimed at the monster's head.

Before its demise, it locked eyes with its conqueror. "You!?" said the beast.

"For Nereus!" said the green man creature. He then tossed the weapon at it and went toward him at lightning speed, making its fatal mark.

"Hey, who are you?" said Obek while Scar went to retrieve the power source and put it in a little sack then into his pocket.

"Hey, guys, we gotta go!" shouted Pragticus.

"Right!" said Adam.

Scar swam to the one who saved them. "Thank you for your assistance. I wish I could stay longer and get acquainted, but we have a battle to finish." He turned to swim back to the surface.

"Wait, are you Scar?" asked the creature with spiky wavy hair that resembled seaweed, his eyes orange mixed with red.

"Why, yes." Scar turned to him.

"I've heard of your great victories against you-know-who. I would be grateful if you'd help me with my affairs?"

"Hey, buddy, didn't you hear? We have to help our men first. They're dying up there!" said Obek.

Scar turned to look at his friend, then turned back to the creature. "What is it?"

"My people are being terrorized by a vicious sea creature so deadly and cunning. His name is Bosberock, and he and his army that…Montorious has commanded him to deploy to take over all of the kingdoms of the sea."

Scar looked down for a moment. "Is there nowhere his power can't reach? Even the sea is his."

"Not if we can help it!" said the creature.

"I'm sorry, you are?" Scar asked.

"Sebawk."

"Right, Sebawk, we just got whooped by you-know-who months ago, and now we're pretty scattered, but once I have more allies, I will surely join the fight with you." Scar reached out his hand to shake Sebawk's hand.

The creature smiled and nodded.

Scar then swam as fast as he could to the surface, sneaking back onto the ship and rejoining the fight as blood was smeared all over the walls.

"Steadfast, men. We can defeat them!" shouted Pragticus.

"Don't give up! Fight, F-I-G-H-T-T-T!" shouted Adam.

A banshee tried lifting up Scar, who quickly reached for his side knife that was gold embedded and stabbed it in her heart. She screamed as she collapsed to the ground. Her body turned to a skeleton, then green mist rose from her.

Veronica sniffed the air and could then sense that the crystal wasn't at its rightful place. "No, impossible!" shouted the headmistress.

"Looking for this?" Scar raised the crystal into the air so she could see it, then quickly put it back in the bag.

"Give it to me!" she said in a booming voice. By now she was all that was left of her sisterhood as the two other serpents were also dead, and the sirens retreated. She cursed out loud, "Damn you,

Jezara!" And she wailed loudly then swooped down, charging toward Scar, tackling him into a wall, choking the life from him. "This is all your doing!" She reeked of seawater stench and other repugnant things in her long flowing black hair. Her eyes were red, and her face was slashed all over as her hands were ice-cold and pruny, grasping his throat tighter now.

Scar tried to reach for his weapon until he saw one of his friends rushing to his aid from behind. He sliced off her head, and green mist then sprayed from the top of her body as he then pushed her body away from Scar. It quickly vanished along with the others.

There was loud thunder then blue lightning from the skies as white balls of light floated in the air, then it was done. The nightmare was over.

Men tossed corpses of the sirens overboard, and robots began cleaning the many decks and halls, fixing broken walls and many other things.

While this was being conducted, Ezra picked up the crystal that was in the bag and gave it to Scar. "I see you acquired the first one for yourself." He smiled.

"Where have you been? Why don't you have a scratch on you?" Scar demanded.

"I...was around. Here, over there. Everywhere." He had his hands in the air as if he were rehearsing a dance, then spun back around, smiling. He then sighed. "Well now, I think I'll go point your robot into the right direction. The next crystal won't be as easy."

Scar slightly laughed. "Oh yeah, I forgot, the last was such a walk in the park."

Ezra just slightly grinned and said, "Aye," then walked off, twirling his cane in the air, dancing in the blood that was on the ground.

Adam then came up beside his friend. "So we're going for the next crystal now, eh?"

"Yup," stated his friend.

"Good 'cause the next one is mine." He then smiled as he playfully punched his friend in the arm and then put an arm over his friend's shoulder as the two began to walk. "I could sure use a bite to eat," said Adam.

Scar laughed "Aye, me too, my friend. Me too."

The two then went off to the kitchen and made a feast for themselves.

CHAPTER 5

Cuxgrog City

"So are you sure you want to do this? It's a high risk that you don't have to take. Someone else can carry the burden," said Scar as he picked up a spoonful of mashed potatoes and gravy. His plate had a giant piece of well-seasoned crispy sirloin with veggies and jumbo garlic butter shrimp. The two made strawberry lemonade as well.

"My friend, whatever hidden power these crystals befall us, I will gladly do so with my brother to whatever end it may also lead us to."

Adam's face became bold. Scar patted his comrade on the back. Adam was noble. There is no greater love than a friend who would lay down his life for a friend (John 15:13).

The ship continued pushing through the cool waters, entering a rocky terrain where there were many mountains. The sun beamed down upon the vessel, and it began to become so hot, men started to dump buckets of water on themselves. They began to pass by giant pillars that were in columns; a clearing was seen as a giant city was ahead.

The crew gazed upon many types of machinery outside surrounding the area and many varieties of vehicles coming to and leaving the port unloading and loading. It was very busy. Men and creatures alike were working. Some were fishing as they made port and docked. Foreigners stood outside with many extravagant things they were waiting to tempt you into buying, waiting like wolves for the kill.

"Ah, Cuxgrog City, how I missed this place. Come, let us settle in and enjoy ourselves for a while. There's no rush to claim what we seek. I have no reason to rush to death so soon," said Ezra as he began to walk halfway down the ramp as it was still stretching itself out onto the cement of the city street.

Scar scratched his head and sighed. "The crew does deserve a time of fun after all we've endured so far," he said aloud to himself, walking down the ramp to his associate.

As the men heard what he said, they cheered, telling everyone else. The thousands of men rushed off to different parts of the city to delight in their own affairs.

Trolls, goblins, and ogres marched in formation in platoons through Cuxgrog and were posted, watching people and arresting monsters and humans alike. One creature was short and had a long tail with an albino-colored scaly skin. He resembled a crocodile with pink eyes with black clothing on. It was arguing with a beast that was some type of rat that was muscular and had an eye patch. The two were involved in a car accident and were accusing the other of foul play. Peacekeepers rushed over trying to break them up.

Scar looked as far as he could to see many bright lights and cars that could fly were in the distance. Ezra tapped him on his shoulder and pointed a way past the city, there were giant gates blocking the entrance into a vast forest. "That's where it is, the next crystal, in an excluded kingdom fortified well by vile giants that reside there, and they have claimed this city to be the rulers of it."

"How on earth do we expect to get there? So many things are here, and looks like the local security wouldn't want them to be bothered," said Adam, who came down the ramp along with the rest of Scar's friends as well as Scout and Floyd.

"Relax, we'll get there. So much stuff happens here on a daily basis. Battles every day with those pigs." Ezra grinned. "The locals will keep them busy in general. Now let us have some fun!" He twirled his staff and walked farther down the ramp and headed straight for the casino.

Scar and his friends exchanged looks, then went their own way to explore this new region as they passed many stores, restaurants, bars, even a place where pretty ladies were trying to lure them in for more relaxing accommodations. This place was a tourist trap with massive buildings that had many giant screens on them of celebrities cooking, selling products, boxing. A three-eyed woman with a cream-colored skin tone with long hair and a dress that sparkled was up ahead, reporting a murder that had happened at someone's house. The family of dog creatures howled loudly as the police carried their family member away in a stretcher.

Scar and his friends found a fancy hotel to stay in that wasn't in the more outlaw part of the city where busy humans and creatures stayed. The beings that were in the lounge gave them funny looks as they sipped their bright, colorful drinks and ate odd-looking food. A group of pretty girls passed by as some weren't human in their group. Adam and his friends turned and smiled. They asked if they wanted to join them at the pool.

"Scar, you got the room, right?" asked Obek as he grinned wide.

Scar shook his head and smiled. "Yeah, guys. Don't get into any trouble now."

They rushed off to the gift shop to buy swimwear.

"Hello there, good chap. How may I be of service?" asked the deskman that was a monster with fur with a pot belly. Scar told him he'd like the biggest room they had. "Oh, marvelous. I'll get your key right for you then." He then handed Scar a basket full of luxury bath soaps that were the shape of medium-sized balls that were in a variety of colors, champagne, chocolates, cheese crackers, and tiny bottles of cologne.

"Wow, thank you, sir." Scar smiled.

The man then slightly nodded his head. "Cheerio now." The manlike creature then walked away and began talking with maids who had come to the counter.

Scout barked happily as he ran off, sniffing plants that were in the hallways and other big open spaces where there were chairs you could sit in and look at the sea. Massive beautiful flowers were also in the lounge area.

"Don't even think about it. You had all that time to relieve your-self outside!" said Scar.

Scout only looked up at his master, sitting and wagging his tail as it sparked off light. Scar then walked over to him, patted his head, and leaned in and kissed his face as Scout licked his friend's face.

"All right, all right. I'll take you once we check out the room."

As they reached their destination, Floyd flew into the room and soared high into the air and went to a massive fish tank and dived in and yanked out a big fish and began eating.

"You're paying for that, my fat furry friend." Scar squinted at the bird.

"Put it on my tab," said Floyd.

Scar rolled his eyes as he gazed upon the massive room that had a kitchen and many hallways that led to rooms. Scout ran to the patio and began to pee as it shot through the bars.

"Hey, what in the world!?" shouted a man below.

"I'm sorry!" shouted Scar as he rushed down to look at the dam-age his pet had caused.

"This isn't what I paid for." He was blindfolded as he wiped his face from the fresh lemon that rained down on him.

There were pretty womenlike creatures with short hair and dark-colored blue skin. One was purple and one a pink color. All were bearing pretty eyes. One was massaging his shoulders as another sat on his lap, dancing on him, and one caressed his feet. They looked up at Scout and giggled. "*Aw*, he's so cute!"

Scout barked and wagged his tail as he popped his head through the bars to look at them. Scar almost turned red as he waved and casually backed up into his room. More people were laughing in the distance in another room, opening wine bottles. He heard people splashing in a pool. Men with animal masks passed by with exotic women who were painted gold with glitter all over them.

"What a freaky place this is." he shook his head and walked back into the room to see what was available on the menu. Room service brought him a smorgasbord of entrées, appetizers, desserts, and drinks. "There, this should be enough for everyone," he said to himself as he put the beverages in the fridge, then made a plate of food for himself and turned on the TV. Times like these, he wished that the current course they were on was just a dream, and he was about to wake up any moment.

Scar used two chopsticks to grasp his sushi and dip it in some type of sauce then another and took a bite. He reached into his pocket and took the crystal out of the bag to examine it for a moment as it glistened. "Please, whatever you do, don't make me look like Floyd," he said aloud to himself as he then watched his friend stare deep into the massive thirty-foot-long fish tank at all the mesmerizing and colorful sea life. His scorpion tail twitched.

There was a loud splash as he plunged underwater again and grasped a king snow crab, then the two went tumbling onto the floor and were tussling. Scout barked loudly and growled as he whipped his tail around and electrocuted the creature, killing it. It fell over on its back and curled its legs the way a spider does.

"I had that," said Floyd as he hopped on the crab's underbelly, ripping off its shell.

"Yeah, sure you did. Good boy, Scout." Scar grinned.

Scout barked happily as he ran over and lay next to his master.

Floyd peeled off the sea creature's limbs and outer shell with precision and then flew over and gave a huge lump of meat to Scout.

Scar put the crystal back in the bag and then into his pocket. He switched through the channels with the remote. "I don't know why I think they'll have anything amusing, no cartoons." He sighed as he stopped on a channel where it was some type of race about to happen with sixty advanced vehicles with monsters and humans. It showed the number of people who were in the race on the left side of the screen in a vertical list.

As the race began, a giant red *X* appeared over their picture when they perished. Scar's face lit up. "Now we're talking. This…I wanna do." He saw at the bottom of the screen there was an advertisement of how you could enter the next race to win millions in cash and a three-year supply of food from any restaurant in the city.

Scar rushed to find something to write with while the race continued. It was an intricate track that was made up of multiple different terrains and obstacles—ice, dessert, rainforest, rock terrain, cavern. The riders were shooting guns at each other from their vehicles and releasing crafty devices from hidden compartments in their bumper.

"Join next time in this *crazy*, out-of-this-galaxy frenzy of mayhem! The annual Ulonax Dresog Prix!"

Scar rushed to work on his device to replicate a design of the appropriate car so he could attempt this challenge.

"Scar, don't get sidetracked like everyone else. We need to focus on the crystals," said Floyd.

"We'll be fine. We can stay here for a while to enjoy what this place has to offer. The war isn't going anywhere."

Floyd ruffled his feathers, then flew over to a bowl of Jell-O and stuffed his face in it.

"Thanks, buddy. I think we all didn't ask for a fish-smelling dessert." Scar gave his friend a disgusted look.

His friend made loud noises as he indulged. "Well, with some of the money, you can always buy Telina some nice things if you don't die a horrible way on the racetrack."

"Thank you deeply for your words of encouragement. They've helped me immeasurably." Scar threw a box of takeout at him. It hit his butt as it bounced off.

"Don't get your panties caught in a frog sag. You'll be good with your wingman with you."

Scar laughed. "Oh yeah, my secret weapon." Scar watched the race as he continued working on the car. A hologram was in the air floating as he switched pieces around, aligning them in order, and picked out tires, spoiler, and other accommodations for looks, then weapons of destruction.

Later, Scar went to find his friends to see how they were doing. It seemed that they were in good hands, so he told them what the room number was and made replica keys for them with his device. He then went back up to the room to rest a while.

He lay in bed, staring up at the ceiling that had a glass covering that showed you a futuristic version of whatever you could imagine. It sank with your mind. He was excited about joining the race next month after they went to the giants' kingdom.

What no one realized was that dark forces were coming to them, and before they would be able to prepare, it'd be too late.

The next morning came swiftly. Scar awoke and opened the shades of his room to see the vast city before him. Busy constituents in the distance were rushing to work. Below, hotel guests were being treated like royalty as waiters brought them loaded trays of food in vast areas, even in the pool!

Our hero did his daily routines, then went to get a bite to eat since when he entered the kitchen, all the food he ordered yesterday was gone. It also was such a mess; trash was everywhere.

"Blasted sea rats. We'll need to get one of the maids to come in," said Scar as he scowled at some of the men who were sprawled out throughout the vast room, snoring loudly. He tried to clean up what he could, then left to venture deeper into Cuxgrog City to see if he could find a place to eat that was a hidden gem.

Scout rushed to his master's side and barked happily as Floyd flew out the door, soaring high into the air and down the hallway.

"Slow down, Floyd, I'm not chasing after you."

The three left the hotel and went down the street down to where they had more exquisite places to eat. Scar first passed businesses opening up as steam from their stores brought heavenly aromas to his senses. There was so much to choose from, he didn't know where to start. Wild animals of the region jumped onto tarps that had food tied to the side and stole shopkeepers' goods. The men spoke in a foreign language, then shouted in English, "I curse your family a thousand times!"

One of the men saw Scar passing and tried to stop him. "Hello, my friend, come sit at Sir Bulagsuraa's Palace. I give you free sample?"

Before he could respond, the man shouted at a woman in a different language as she rushed out and handed Scar a lizard that was battered in a breaded seasoning and deep-fried.

"Oh, thank you." Scar smiled at her as she blushed and looked down, then rushed back to work with the other men and women.

"Ah, you like her, my friend? I give you good deal on her as well. Half price since she's my cousin." The man grinned as he threw an arm around Scar's neck.

"*Yeah*, I'll pass. Thank you for the food though." Scar walked away as the man was still shouting to him many silly things, trying to get him to change his mind as he took a bite of the reptile cuisine.

Floyd perched himself onto his friend's shoulder, leaning in to get a bite of this delectable snack. "My my, we have to stay here longer. I think I can make a living here being a notable food tester."

Scar laughed and shook his head as he tore a piece off and tossed it to Scout. They walked for a bit longer till they saw a secluded spot where there was an ocean view from a built-in restaurant on the mountainside. There was also a man-made waterfall that you could sit out in a fancy boat and eat or at a table overlooking the pool of water.

He walked up the steep steps that led to it and sat down. A man approached him immediately and handed him a menu and told him the specials. Surprisingly, the food portions were hefty. They had a menu also for other life-forms where Floyd ordered from and found something for Scout as well while Scout was occupied staring at giant pretty sea creatures—fish, turtles, and other ancient things that swam below since the glass beneath the establishment was a giant fish tank. He pressed his face on the glass enclosure.

While Scar awaited his food, he noticed a familiar face coming up the steps. It was the girl who gave him the appetizer in the market. She was dressed differently now, more like an outlaw, wearing a leather jacket and boots, and she had a sword on her back with two laser guns on both sides of her waist. Her hair was down, and her bright hazel eyes were glistening from the sun.

"Seems like you've finally known there's more out there than just Telina, huh?" said Floyd as he pressed his face against Scar's cheek, trying to be funny as he nudged him with him with his left wing.

"Shut up, Floyd. She is gorgeous, that's all. I wonder if she will recognize me," he said to himself aloud.

She walked to the counter of the bar as another woman approached from behind it and smiled. "Hey, girl! Nice move you did at the prix last month. I knew you were going to win again. That asshole ex of yours always thinks he will."

The two laughed.

"Yeah, he's a clown, and he only wanted one thing, and he ain't even get that!"

The two laughed even harder.

"Go on and get a seat, and I'll fix up your usual, boo."

The girl from the market smiled and walked over to where Scar was and happened to sit at a table across from them. She pulled out some type of device with lit-up holograms, and she tapped one and began watching a news feed of something, giggling out loud, typing back to people as other stuff was commencing on the other side of the floating TV screen where people were doing antics.

"Looks like you'll have competition to compete now. There's no way you can beat her. You'll be too busy drooling the whole time," said Floyd.

Scar glared at his friend. "If you don't be quiet, you'll be swimming with the fishies!"

Scout at that moment barked and began to pounce on the glass, trying to play with a baby puffer fish.

"No, relax, boy," said Scar.

This made the girl look up from her device. She squinted her eyes, then grinned as she had one foot propped up. "Fancy meeting you here. I'm sorry my brother harassed you. He does that to potential cash cows, always playing matchmaking."

Scar smiled. "Wait, your bro? He said—"

She cut him off. "My brother will say anything that doesn't make sense." She rolled her eyes and smiled.

Scar slightly smiled and quickly stood up. "Please join me." He pulled the chair out that was beside him as the young woman approached and sat down. "So, you're a racer, huh? Nice. I was looking into competing this time around."

"Oh really? You think you can handle me, huh? My moves are nothing you've ever had before." She grinned slightly.

Scar began to slightly sweat. "Is it getting hot to you?" He picked up his drink filled with ice.

"Pull yourself together, you're embarrassing me," said Floyd at that moment.

Scar threw a napkin that was wrapped around silverware at him, and this made him back up and fall off the table.

"Why I never…" He ruffled his feathers as he sat beside Scout, who looked at him and turned his head to the side and licked his face.

"Your friends seem sweet," she said.

"Yeah, they aight." Scar slightly grinned. "I think you'd be a great teacher to help me not get killed out there on the track. Is there a place you could show me the ropes?"

She smiled. "Yeah, I know a place. I think you'll like it a lot. Won't go easy on you though, still have to be the best around here," she teased.

"Oh, you can be the best wherever you go," said Scar.

She made a funny scrunched-up expression that was cute but still broke a smile. "I'm sorry, my name is Maria."

"Scar."

The two shook hands. Their food had finally arrived, and Maria's friend had brought it. She set her friend's plate down, then looked at Scar then stuck her tongue out at her friend and made a silly expression. "If he has a friend, let me know." She then rushed back off and tended to things.

"Just ignore her," Maria said as she casually drank her drink that was a shade of pink with sliced fruit on the side of the tall glass.

They talked for a few hours, then made their way to this place she was fond of to escape the crazy city. It led to a more off-road, back-world area. Scar used his device to retrieve his new vehicle.

Maria looked impressed. "Wow, I could get used to a man like you, already handy."

Scar laughed as he opened the car door. She hopped in as his friends hopped in the little spot in the back enough for some luggage. Maria told him of what controls did what and what would be best to use first and how many laps there would be. The next race was actually in two months, so this gave him more time to get acquainted with his new friend Maria and, most of all, train for the race.

While common crime ran a flood in the city, the many pre-cincts that were throughout were overwhelmed, and Scar and his friends offered to help. Of course, crime syndicate lords didn't like this. Surely they'd pay for him to be taken out in the prix so he wouldn't further ruin their business.

Scar drove on many intricate tracks that were created by local folk for kids to be out there instead of soliciting near their establishments. Scar gripped the steering wheel and drifted over a body of water that was on the track from a hard rain, dodging other obstacles. Large guns came out from the sides of his vehicle that destroyed obstacles, and he rode up ramps that soared him in the air far and landed back down into another place that had ice, so he changed his tires entering an ice cavern going through tunnels, down steep icy roads. Sensors went off that dropped giant ice balls that he had to avoid. He entered a bog terrain next, then a lava region with multiple volcanoes, and then a tunnel that took you underwater, and you could see terrifying creatures on both sides of the protective glass.

There was even a beach theme region with massive whirlpools of sand that could suck you in.

"Nice work. You've improved a lot," said Maria, who was driving beside him in her exotic, flashy enhanced vehicle as she then floored it and pressed the NO_2 and left him in the dust.

"You know, why don't we just work together? You can just join us when we leave and join our journey."

"And die for this awful planet? No thanks, I'd rather save up enough and leave this place, try my luck on a different planet, maybe even another galaxy."

"You have so much talent that we could use to do so much good, and I—I mean, *we* all would appreciate your company, and maybe who knows on our travels, we might just visit another planet, and you'll realize that Vospheron isn't all that bad. You really just need to leave Cuxgrog!" said Scar through the radio system in his car to his friend.

She sighed. "You're right, maybe I'll come with you guys…if you ever can beat me in this virtual simulation system!" she teased as she went even faster now.

But Scar had been studying her moves for weeks, and he finally knew how to outmaneuver her. He took a shortcut through a muddy road that was bumpy and had potholes and also geysers of colorful water sprouting out. As he kept driving, he saw a tunnel ahead then a spiral road and a ramp farther out.

He pressed a button as he flew back in his seat. "Ow, Floyd! If you're going to be on my shoulder, refrain from digging your claws into my skin!" Scar briefly looked up at his friend, scowling.

"Hey, I'm not used to us soaring off like a wild Varsetrax."

Scar shook his head. "You wouldn't be able to handle my world's roller coasters then, that's for sure."

Floyd began to clean his feathers and other parts of himself.

"If you're going to do that, then please get off!" Scar swerved the vehicle, and his friend soared in the air and hit the window. Scar saw the ramp ahead, but all of a sudden, a huge obstacle appeared out of nowhere in the middle of the road. He pressed a button to release the guns, but it was too late. He shot a few rounds but smashed through the large sculpture as the car spun, going up the ramp, soaring through the air, landing back on the road of yet another different terrain, and the finish line was only a few feet away. He tried to get a hold of the vehicle to get back in position, but saw someone approaching from the side. It was Maria!

She came to the side of the car and rolled down her window. She was grinning. Her hair was in a ponytail. "Wow, I think that time, you almost actually had me."

Scar rolled his eyes. "Yeah, I would have if my friend here wasn't being a pain."

She laughed. "Ooh, blame it on him again, huh? If I weren't mistaken, I think you could have beaten me by now, you just don't want me to get hurt in the process," said Maria in a cute voice.

Scar slightly smiled as he looked into her eyes. "Is that right."

At that moment, six vehicles that were all different designs and colors pulled up. A tall young adult got out of a purple car with a green intricate design on it with green brake calibers and a massive spoiler on the trunk.

"Look what we have here. I finally found you, love," said a broad man with tattoos. He had black hair and a massive knife on his side.

Maria rolled her eyes. "What do you want, Cal?"

"Oh, don't be stuck-up, as if I were here to see you." He then glared at Scar in his ruined vehicle. "Oh, looks like it won't be any problem kicking your scum self off the track. You've done my job for me." He and his friends laughed.

Scar just gave him a look.

"I hope you'll be ready in time so I can have an actual challenge this prix because I promise you, it'll surely be a blast," said Cal as he then looked at his ex and puckered his lips up, making a smooching sound, then he spun around and put his hand in the air and pointed a finger in the air and twirled it around, giving the signal to move out.

They yelled barbarically and took off down the road.

Maria pulled out her device as she shut off the simulation, and the road morphed back to a regular dirt road that was not as masterly intricate. "Don't mind him, he always thinks that newcomers in the race are pushovers and can be scared not to engage." She smiled.

"I'm not worried about him." Scar slightly grinned as Maria chuckled slightly. "Say, I've had enough for one day. Let's go get a bite to eat?" asked Scar as she took her hair out of the ponytail and spun around all elegant, walking away.

"Let's go then."

Scar hopped out of his vehicle without opening the door as he briefly watched her walk away.

"Boy, Scar, I know you love Telina, but damn!"

Scar shook his and laughed briefly. "Floyd, come on now." He began to walk away from his destroyed car as Floyd flew out of the vehicle and perched upon his shoulder.

They briefly went back to the hotel room to pick up Scout, who was patiently awaiting his master's return.

Maria took Scar to a place where you ordered the food, and you had a small firepit in the middle of the table and you cooked the food yourself. It was an all-you-can-eat menu of meats!

"Nice gig you picked. You sure know me well in only a few months," said Scar as he took a bite of his double chocolate volcano cake that had come with a generous serving of vanilla bean ice cream.

"Well, any woman knows a way to a man's heart is his stomach." She lifted her glass of wine and took a sip.

Adam and the rest of Scar's closets friends were out volunteering to help keep the streets at peace with the police for a short while longer while Scar enjoyed the rest of his night. He had to prepare diligently for the next grand prix that was only just days away.

Meanwhile, particular forces were closing in on his position and would soon bring even more chaos in this already accursed city.

The day of the annual Unolax Dresog Prix was finally here, and it was a very exciting day for many. Everyone wanted to be at peace for one day just to watch fellow neighbors and outsiders battle it out for their amusement.

It was nearly sunrise, and it was slightly foggy. Scar gripped his steering wheel as he looked outside his massive front window that had other holograms on the screen to his right. The massive track was inside a huge dome that was in a simulation system consisting of twelve different areas and twenty-five laps total. Some riders leaned out of their vehicle, egging the crowd on to show them the love and attention they rightfully deserved, as if they're only there to see them.

A massive contraption was in the air for all to see, which consisted of multiple screens flashing different clips of racers for you to see your favorite riders for a few minutes, then switched to someone else. Another smaller robot with a TV screen for a face hovered in the air, flying around with its feet as thrusters. Hot air blew from beneath it, and a man was on the screen talking to the drivers.

Creatures and humans were selling their scrumptious delectables from companies, things from their shops, and homemade delights. Kids pulled on their parents' clothes and cried asking for things, while others pouted and demanded, throwing things at concessioners who walked past. Creatures handed humans odd-looking things that were still alive drenched in some type of sauce in a tray; others were given meat in fried breading with a special type of condiment unknown. Some had tarantulas and other creepy crawlers cooked and sautéed right in front of them. Thankfully, there were some known foods as well for the faint of heart. Massive cheeseburgers, loaded fries, giant beer cheese pretzels, buckets of chocolate chip cookies. It was a festival! But I must say, how could they all eat when people were about to die?

A massive group of creatures that were dressed in full Cuxgrog prix fan attire fought over seats and who was going to win, and security rushed over to break up this fiasco. One was a woman who had a pretty skin tone and long hair that she used to pick up two of the men who were fighting. "Now now, boys, play nice." She had a massive gun holstered on her back and other heinous weapons on her person. Scar's friends were in the stadium as well, shouting and cheering.

At that moment, a massive man that was half a monster sat right next to Obek. In his abnormal hands was a huge tray of food. He pressed a button on the side of his chair, and a table came out in front of him. Obek was squished between his friends and this brute.

"Excuse me, but can you go somewhere else? I have no room," said Obek.

The man glared down at him. "Hey, buddy, is there a problem? Leave me alone. I came to watch the game like everybody else. I'm a loyal tax-paying resident of this city."

Obek rolled his eyes. "Oh, you're one of those guys" he mumbled under his breath as he nudged Pragticus in the side to move over.

"What was that, boy?" asked the massive creature who had giant tusks and a giant pet of some kind across his neck.

"Nothing," replied Obek.

"That's what I thought," said the man in triumph as he began eating his fill of the horde of food he'd brought. He dug in his coat pocket and pulled out a bottle of alcohol and poured it in his drink.

"*Welcome*, humans, goblins, ghouls, monsters, and other lovely menaces to society to the annual Unolax Dresog Prix! You're in for a mad day filled with laughter, excitement, and explosions galore! For those who paid extra to be in the splash zone where limbs and blood may land, get ready to feast, you grotesque beasts of the night!"

A system of colorful lights came down from the ceiling that resembled streetlights. It made loud noises, flashing different colors as everyone revved their engines. Finally it was green, and everyone took off like rockets, dodging obstacles, ramming into each other.

Of course the pawns went first, the foolish ones who had no business joining such a carnaged event but were adrenaline junkies and had to complete a bucket list challenge that unfortunately cost them their lives. No one was able to use their weapons until they were at least thirty minutes in. It made no difference as most of these racers were experts and had won races from their own regions and had come to dominate this one as well.

Tires were blown out by weapons and soared into the air, hitting other racers' vehicle's as some flipped a few times and crashed into structures, catching on fire shortly after. Some skilled racers spun their cars around and shot at other oncoming racers who were behind them, going toe to toe with one another. Although the armor on the enhanced roadsters was superb, they could only withstand so much.

Maria dodged the many obstacles that were before her as Scar was only a few cars behind her.

"Get 'em, get 'em!" shouted Floyd, who was strapped into some type of equipment that resembled a car seat for a baby, and he had a helmet on.

"Be quiet, you! I know what I'm doing. Don't distract me, or you'll get us both killed!" said Scar, who had an intricate driver's helmet on with an algid color design. His keen eyes kept straight ahead on the road, dodging to the left then the right, passing racers through tunnels and up ramps that soared him in the air then back down onto a new track where weird and other terrifying contraptions were also deployed randomly if you happened to stumble upon them.

This barbaric race was an endless round-and-round loop of your worst nightmare. Nothing prepared him for this in his training. Scar shot weapons at some racers only to demobilize them, only acting out to the final strike if necessary. Many racers catapulted farther by using their NO_2 capabilities, while few were destroyed when they lost control when turning. Everyone else drifted with ease around winding turns that were meant to be their grave.

These prestigious racers drove over vast domains that were covered in mostly water, so they quickly changed their cars into aquatic capabilities in seconds as they submerged below into the water for a few miles on a track. Around them was all kinds of creepy sea life. Schools of giant colorful fish swam above them, and stone hammer crabs the size of semitrucks tried clamping onto vehicles. Oncoming racers fought for their lives from beasts of the sea as well as their opponents.

"Still glad you tagged along?" Scar teased as he briefly looked over at his friend, who was already looking at him, squinting his eyes. "I hate you," he said.

Scar laughed. "We'll be out of here in no time, and I'll beat Maria!" Scar pressed his NO_2 button and sped ahead, swerving past floating giant pieces of debris that floated in front of him randomly, and giant hammer crabs fell onto the track from being killed by other people.

"Now he'd be good smothered in a bowl of butter!" said Floyd, who stared at the corpse, and his stomach began to growl.

Finally they saw light up ahead. There was a steep ramp, and many racers were already going up it, but not before going through an intricate loop with swirls that conjoined and connected with another loop where two racers had an unfortunate demise, colliding into one another. Scar safely got out from the sea tomb and was right beside his friend, who looked over at him. She wore an enhanced helmet as well. The two were neck to neck, both driving exception- ally well while they drifted across bodies of water and dodged hungry massive sharks that sprouted out of pools of water.

While our hero was about to make it out of this water terrain, another rider shot him at the side of his car. He'd come from the side of the track in hiding near where pool of water was.

Our friend's car flipped once and hit the side of the railing hard. His systems were shaking, and a man came online, telling him the results of damages while another vehicle pulled up to him that was bright red with silver trim and black roof. It was Cal, that bastard. He began shooting at him again while Scar was about to move; his car was also fixing damages at the same time.

Cal was still being ruthless trying to eliminate him, not caring about the race. This seemed more personal. Another type of creature latched onto Cal's vehicle at that very moment and tried pulling him into the water. He revved his engine and pressed a few buttons as immense fire came out from the rear, putting the beast aflame.

This was Scar's chance to leave, but before doing so, he shot lasers then other guns that extracted out and giant bullets came out. The integrity of his fellow contester's car was strong. He also dropped little spike balls from the rear to take him out as he sped off onto the next track.

This rodeo went on for hours until finally, they were on the last lap, and there were twenty-five racers left. Giant snow boulders soared in the air, and snow whispered as it covered the windows of the racers. The road was icy, but they had spike tires to best this cunning track.

Scar was now in the lead as Maria was now behind a few cars, fighting with a few other racers. He scaled up the mountain, entering a glass tube of some sort that boosted his speed and shot him out the other side back onto the track. He briefly looked below to see giant beasts swarm together, roaring and gnashing their teeth, hoping that someone would make a fatal mistake. A few other racers finally caught up with him, shooting out different-colored lasers from behind. Scar pressed a button that shot out bullets that sounded as if a cannon had gone off, and these were aimed at those behind him. He stayed on his current course.

There was a road to the left of him that seemed like a shortcut but was very dark and winding. "I'll have to risk it," he said aloud to himself, swerving onto the exclusive track. He turned on his headlights that beamed halogen, and all of a sudden, medium-sized creatures dropped down from the sides of the cavern and started gnawing on the outside of his vehicle. He quickly electrocuted them off, but more kept coming. On top of that, other racers followed him in, shooting at him again. This time it was a relief; this plague of cretins was an army!

Scar saw the exit ahead while he briefly looked above to see thousands more of the monsters come rampaging down. He had to hurry! Scar pressed his NO_2 button, but it still needed to recharge! He pressed his foot on the gas pedal, almost breaking it, it seemed, as he shot multiple types of weapons at them from his armada of guns toward this horde that gave him his window of opportunity. Of course, this gave his rivals one as well, but a few weren't so lucky. There was a two-mile stretch left that they were on high above the ground on giant stone pillars that kept the bridge sturdy, while snow still fell and ice was still on the road. There were giant spike balls on chains that swung from above and other contraptions that could crush you from above, and other giant guns that were mounted were being shot at you from hidden positions.

"Geez, it's as if they don't want anyone to win," said Scar aloud as his screen on the right side was showing the track and the finish line ahead. He was scaling up a steep ramp now then down the other side as giant mounds of snow piles suddenly began to appear out of nowhere to desist their current course. Scar managed to maneuver past them as he shot through the last one and burst through it. As snow flew everywhere, the crowd cheered and threw things in the air.

Scar went in between these two massive pillars that were decked out and had flames above. As he went past them, loud horns blared, and confetti dropped from the ceiling of the dome.

"It looks like we have a winner! The new *comer*, *Scar!* This is rarely ever seen! Stay tuned for the next riveting battle domain soon!"

Scar got out of his vehicle as people and monsters alike cheered while he made his way to the victor's arena. Creatures and humans alike who were overseers congratulated him and handed him prizes that came in an advanced-looking card filled with his earnings and a bright gold trophy.

The other racers were now in the assembly area. Some got out and bickered with one another. Scar rushed over to see if he could find Maria, who was already out of her car, leaning against the hood with her helmet under her left arm. She smiled. "Well done, new-comer! I can't believe you actually bested me."

Scar walked closer toward her. "Hmm, I have a feeling that you let me win." Scar looked into her bright eyes.

She briefly looked down, then looked back up and cracked a cute smile. "Now what gave you that idea?"

The two stargazed for a moment when there was a sudden loud bang outside the dome that shook the entire stadium.

"Ahem, may I have your attention, everyone! It appears that we have an army coming into Cuxgrog City to take the one named Scar. Thank you for ruining our lives. Please, everyone, if you happen to get hurt by falling equipment, don't die until you are off of Dresgog property, thank you, goodbye, and oh yes, run for your lives!" shouted the announcer on the speakers.

Many people and creatures were already rushing to the multiple exits, swarming like herds of cattle out of the stadium. The dome was being bombarded with multiple bombs.

"Well, looks like you brought the war here now. I have no choice but to go with you," said Maria as she punched Scar in his shoulder and put her helmet back on and hopped back into the car.

"I'll round up my friends and meet you at the gates where the giants live. Now's a good time to get what we came for before they take wind," said Scar.

She nodded then shot at a wall and sped out of the dome.

Floyd fluttered his wings. "Oh boy, we're in for it now."

Scar hopped back into his car to quickly retrieve Scout from his hotel room, but the streets were filled with chaos as many tried to make it home, and the local policemen and military of the massive city were battling it out with men in enhanced armor with battle masks on and had frightening creatures at their disposal. Scar tried to maneuver through as fast as he could, shooting at the armored men who quickly were fortifying blockades.

"Damn, it's those blasted men who were in league with Xsuss," said Scar aloud as he finally made it to his destination. The fancy area of the city had not yet been touched by the invaders, so military was preparing with Scar's friends and a few garrisons of soldiers from his regime while the rest were back upon the ship waiting to leave as others were stuck in the red zone.

Scar rushed inside the hotel back to his room and got his friend. Scout ran down the hall, and his hairs began to prickle up like quills; he sensed something was coming. Adam and the rest were below talking with giant creatures that were special ops police teams, and the military had big guns they were mounting up at multiple spots.

Guests in the hotel were screaming, running back to their rooms to hide as if they'd be safe.

Another gentleman was complaining to management about the current course of action and that they wished to be extracted immediately since their vacation was now ruined, and he threatened to sue. Other women who wore fancy attire were yelling at busboys to give them drinks and food they'd ordered.

Scar told his friends where he was going. Before they left with him, Pragticus ordered more men to stay and help assists the military and police while a few left with them to face the giants. Everyone hopped in the car, and he pressed his NO_2 to make up time while the rest commandeered a local military vehicle. It'd be only hours till the enemy was at their position and no telling how long it'd take to obtain the crystal from these foul giants.

Finally they arrived at the massive bolted gates. It took a lot of firepower to break them down from both Maria's arsenal and Scar's on their subcompacts. Their weapons were steaming hot with smoke. Everyone walked over the destroyed pieces of the gate and rushed in. It was a fairly easy straight shot, for who would be foolish enough to go where they'd be lunch?

There was a lengthy forest to get through while creatures never before seen resided in there but were harmless. A massive fortress was up ahead, a long stone bridge connected to it. There, no one was in sight.

They quickly went across and scaled over the walls, rushing past giant tables, brooms, weapons, and massive dead things from previous battles and buildings that still needed mending.

"Ick, they sure don't tidy things up, lazy swines," said Maria, who fixed her hair into a ponytail.

They stumbled upon a massive hole in the wall that led below down to a dark-lit area with massive steps; they had to be careful. They entered in while a sudden strong draft picked up and whiffed a peculiar smell that caught their senses. The farther they proceeded, the fouler it smelled. They could hear loud echoing below that rang through the area like raging bats.

Scar and his group went in a little farther and jumped from the stairs off to a ledge that had many boulders that they hid behind. Smoke arose from a huge pot that bubbled many colors.

"Brothers! Come, let us rejoice once more our tenth century of the sacred…" The being spoke in a booming voice in a different language.

Scar climbed up a giant rock, and once he got to the top, his eyes grew wide. Dozens of sixteen-foot massive beasts were walking around. They had turnips covering their bodies, and some were dressed in full armor. Giant weapons were hanging to the right on a wall. All the monsters were listening to what one creature had to say.

"Now I shall bring forth the crystal!" He raised something that shone bright that was embedded into a weapon. "Behold!" He aimed it near the crowd as the grotesque bottom dwellers raised their hands into the air, embracing the powerful energy that engulfed the area, only affecting them as it changed them into more horrible ways than before. Spikes sprouted on their elbows and down their backs, some grew multiple eyes, tails, arms, and some blew fire out of their mouths.

The beasts cheered.

"We are gods! Now we can surely overthrow Montorious and his legions!" said one of the giants triumphantly.

The room then became silent.

"Don't be a fool. Remember your place. I should rip off your head for such insolence. Our city and the inhabitants that dwell here pay us handsomely. Right here is all we need," said the head giant while the creature that spoke foolishly knelt before him, begging for forgiveness. "Our job is to smite any stragglers that stumble upon here from the most recent battle and…those bloody pirates."

The head giant spat while he spoke and gritted his teeth.

"Those barbaric sea rats, so defiant all because of their code only to themselves."

The monsters laughed maniacally.

At that moment, Scar's friend climbed up some boulders as well. Some men who tagged along had bows and arrows ready, awaiting his signal. Maria was about to unholster her weapon and shoot the leader of these brutes right between the eyes. Scar motioned hand movements toward her not to.

"Once the arrows start soaring, I'll grab what we came for in a cinch," said Floyd.

Scar rolled his eyes. "You think it'll be that easy?" Scar turned his head to talk to his friends for a moment, but once he turned back, his feathery robust friend was gone. "Okay, men, aim for their eyes and neck. The leader's mine."

A soldier handed him a bow and arrow.

"On my mark."

Floyd swiftly flew behind pillars in the cover of darkness.

Scar gave a hand signal, and arrows soared through the air, raining down like the walls of Jericho while screams ignited from giants as many hid behind pillars.

"Grab our shields!" shouted one as Scar's arrow struck him in the head, then another and another. Thirty more after pierced him all over, then he was dead. Another came out of hiding, roaring and swinging his weapon violently, deflecting dozens of arrows.

Floyd swooped below and plucked the crystal out of the weapon it was incased in with his raptor claw, then grasped it in his talons.

"No, stop him!" their leader shouted, livid, his face red, veins from his neck bulging out while his brethren blew fire and ice from their mouths to stop Floyd. "Not that way, you fools, over there! Careful, you imbeciles, you'll destroy the crystal!"

The giants began throwing massive spears at the rocks to impale our heroes, but each time they hit a boulder, a massive chunk broke off, as if there was dynamite stuck to it.

"Hurry back to the ship!" shouted Pragticus.

The group quickly made their way off the ledge and toward the exit where some beasts were already waiting for them. Some were smashed as others blasted their way through helping each other up the steps while many gave covering fire. Maria and her weapons were a big help, and the bombs Scar retrieved from his device and were thrown stuck to the walls and brought down massive chunks of structure, assisting their escape and keeping their lovely house greeters occupied.

By this time, Scar and his crew were already out of their domain and back into Cuxgrog City where they had to fight their way to the bay. In many places, people still drank and ate, relaxing like any other given day. Many futuristic soldiers were positioned throughout battling local gangs as well, while Scar fought many unique formidable men and women who bore Montorious's mark on their armor while the giants finally broke free, and loud horns were blown.

Everyone stopped fighting in the city and looked to the giants' lair past the trees that began falling down like dominos, and giants began charging to the city. Hundreds were riding massive beasts that had three tails, covered in fur, tusks, and three eyes with sharp teeth.

Everyone began fighting once more; many of the creatures and humans in the gangs shouted cocky words since the giants were coming to their aid, they assumed, but instead, they killed all in their path, even the armored men.

Rulugof, who was at a nearby bar with his men waiting for his units to get the job done, heard the giants outside and rushed outside and demanded what they were doing. "Have you lost your sense of reason, or are you all too dumb to comprehend who's on your side, you disgusting creatures?" said Rulugof, who had the creatures that were chained on the ship at that moment pour out around him and his team trickled out.

"Let's end them all now, boss. They are an eyesore," said Cyrox.

"Hell yeah!" said Jaxer, throwing one arm over another one of his comrades.

Residents of the city screamed, trying to hide or make it back to their homes, while others rushed to the Cuxgrog airways airport in masses to escape the battle.

"I wonder if this is a bad time to say I'm in the mood for some ass," said Damaris.

Suddenly, a man swatted him on the back of his helmet hard. "Shut up and focus and take the safety off your weapon," said Lero.

"Oh, whatever, like we need it. We all have powers anyways, that's why we're the Daemon guard elite!" Damaris shouted, raising one hand in the air and balling it into a fist.

Any solider wearing their fancy armored getup who was close by shouted, "Hail the Daemon guard!"

"I'm ready to go. Scar is probably long gone, and we'll have to chase him," said Aris with a sigh. He had his advanced sniper rifle aimed at a giant's eye as their leader, Rulugof, still spoke with the giant king.

The giants stopped their assault and listened.

"Now you've just killed fifty of my men being lunatics. Now I need fifty of your heads, or I'll just kill you all right now. The agreement to work with you things was Lord Victor's choice, one of Xsuss's allies, but we honor his death by agreeing with his terms still, but I will not stand idly by and let you kill my men."

At that moment, his team raised massive weapons to kill them all, but instead, they randomly shot at a bunch of them and killed them as they fell off the furry beasts they were upon.

The head giant just growled and didn't say a word after they were done, and smoke steamed from their guns.

"There, now that's better. Now you can get back to work doing whatever it was and be the good little lapdogs you are for our supreme Lord Montorious," said Rulugof, glaring at the head giant.

By this time the streets were cleared of innocent bystanders and just equal opportunists were still at large.

The leader of the towering monsters then took one last look at the futuristic men, then took off down the street, shaking buildings and turning over cars and such in his wake while his army swarmed behind him.

"Ah, such a repugnant smell they carry," Rulugof said aloud. As he was about to step back into his threshold, a man passed by carrying a soldier in his arms who had half of his body.

"Such loss today," said the man as he sighed, setting down his comrade, then looked up at Rulugof. "Days of suffering have grabbed me!" The man had despair in his eyes.

Rulugof just stared at the man for moment, then turned around and went back into the bar and sat down to have a drink. His mind raced about his own brother, Euu'nn-ralla, back home and the evil contract his king chose to bind with Montorious. He grasped his glass so hard, it shattered.

A few men in black armor with pink-colored designs on it wearing battle masks stood up and walked over to their leader. "Sir, are you okay?" one asked.

Rulugof reached over the counter and grabbed a bottle and began guzzling it, then stopped and set it down. He then looked straight ahead. "Never better, Yuka."

By this time, Scar and his men were close to the dock, and Adam was fighting with Scout. They had gotten pinned down, and Floyd was still flying with the crystal while the beasts tried throwing rocks at him to stop him from getting away.

Scar awaited the rest of his friends at the dock while his robots started the engines and other people manned weapons on the ship's thousands of decks. The ship also began to push out while the rope was still attached to the pier.

Adam and Scout made it to the deck and jumped aboard before it was too far out. Scar untied the rope, still waiting for his friend, and Maria. who stood behind him, tried to urge him to get aboard. "He'll come, but we need to get on too."

He finally listened to reason, and the two took hold of the rope that was hanging and climbed up. Scar stood on the deck and watched to see his friend flap his wings for dear life, exhausted as his friend laid his arm out, and he safely landed on his arm and dropped the crystal in his other hand.

The ship then put up a force field to protect them from the many giant stones and other things being thrown at them while the monsters shouted and cursed, saying dreadful things.

The head giant pushed through his men and stared at Scar from afar.

"Pelgdon, what do we do now?" one asked.

"We summon the Meoncha, and we get my crystal back!" he shouted as he pushed through his brethren and went back into the enfumed chaotic city of Cuxgrog.

CHAPTER 6

Jasper's Return

"THAT BIG OAF! HOW DOES HE NOT see that I am ready!?" shouted Jasper. He was carving something on the wall of his ship while few of the blue tigers from Fee'uun that survived were prowling the deck along with his small band of elite men that Montorious had given him. "That bastard Tambada thinks he's so smart. I'll show that arrogant, pompous…" He grinned wide.

Where is the last crystal? It's as if something or someone was shielding its presence. Glory and respect shall be given to who wields it.

Jasper then looked down, pondering. It was night, and the moon and stars glistened. The air was crisp while cool breezes blew incessantly. His long black hair covered his face. It would be a fortnight till they reached their destination. While he wasted away in his own despair and selfish desires of the flesh, his agony of defeat weighed heavy upon him.

Oh, the poor lad, thinking the world revolved around him, that it'd become intermittent for a moment, and everyone would give him the praise he deserved. Do you feel sorry for him? Can you discern his pain? Do you too long to be noticed by man, also becoming deceived by a trap of your own making? (Galatians 1:10, ERV). Can you not blame Jasper for choosing the winning side? I have also been a foolish example of the corruption we allow ourselves to propagate in with the desires this world has to offer. Let us learn from our mistakes before we too become far too gone like our dear friend Jasper (Romans 12:2, ERV).

But who knows, maybe there is still hope for him, although his own arrogance becomes him. Maybe he'll get exactly what he wants, like the saying, "Gain the world and lose your soul."

"Jasper, how long will we pillage these feeble towns searching for what cannot be found unless it wants to be? It longs for its true master," said one of his comrades.

Jasper then stabbed the knife deep into the wood of the ship. "We will continue on our current course until we have success, Kinoki."

At that moment, it began to rain abruptly. The man just gave him a look, then shook his head. "Shall we perish like your previous team?" Kinoki said lividly, then stormed off.

Jasper then stood up and walked to the other side of the ship, gazing upon how the rain gingerly fell down elegantly onto the water, then disappearing once it touched it.

He closed his eyes and inhaled the fresh seawater air, then exhaled, trying to clear his mind. All of a sudden, a voice began to speak to him. "I can use you for my will, give you powers you've only dreamt of. Denounce Montorious and join me."

My, my, what does this remind you of? There is a similar situation when Yeshua was fasting in the desert, and the evil one came to try and tempt him (Matthew 4:8–11).

Jasper's eyes shot open, and he used one hand to wipe the damp hair from his face. "Who said that?" he asked, slowly reaching for his sword.

A white orb emerged from beneath the water. As that happened, lightning struck the water and lit the ocean. You could briefly spot terrifying sea creatures deep in the seabed, lurking, waiting for their next meal.

"So what shall it be, Jasper, descendant of Thasbamuln?"

The white orb suddenly began to grow into the shape of a transparent body and eyes that looked like the galaxy itself.

"Who are you? You are brave to speak such words of treason that can end your life."

The figure laughed. "The dead do not fear such things. Well, limited, I should say." He raised a hand into the air and balled it into a fist. "Imprisoned." He squinted his eyes.

"So what, do you want me to release you, eh?" Jasper asked.

"No, when I am free, I want worthy allies, and you will be much appreciated. I see greatness in you. All you have to do is tell me your master's entire layouts in his kingdom." He grinned wide.

Jasper just looked at the odd creature for moment. "You do know he truly rules this world, all of Vospheron."

The creature chuckled. "Oh, my boy, do you know who really rules this world? Far darker beings than him that lie in the depths of the darkest of night, waiting to reclaim this world for our—I mean, *their* own. Let me ask you something. Have you even been to the other part of this vast world yet? You say he rules it, but how do you know for sure? There's so much you don't know. There are many beings that are enfumed on this planet that are his adversaries, and so certain persons have been assigned to…expunge their time on this beautiful planet. Jasper, there's so much for you elsewhere, beyond this place. You have a destiny to fulfill with old friends from the past who were great leaders, greater than you-know-who," said the monster.

This all deeply confused Jasper, and it was a lot to take in. "I'll have to think about your offer."

The eerie transparent being made a look of dissatisfaction upon his face. "Fine, take your time. I do hope you change your mind." The figure then slowly began to sink back into the black water and disappeared.

If you were quiet, you could hear the low moaning and groaning of the sea beasts that dwelled below. Luckily, everyone was down below feasting, and the blue saber tigers were asleep. If anyone had overheard the slightest bit of betrayal in his breath, they'd kill him and toss his mangled body overboard. He was terrified of that very thing.

So the tables have turned. Raka wants to overthrow his partner. What a surprise. Though his rival had Xsuss's army and his other evil kings at his beck and call, what does Raka possess that can make him accomplish such an ordeal?

Shortly after his discussion with the ghoul, Jasper decided to go rest for a bit, and that was when he was haunted by all the innocent lives he'd slain.

While the days passed, the warriors of this voyage continued their ghastly search for the crystal as ordered while brave men tried to protect their villages, failing in the end. Only six men were assisting Jasper in this cleansing of proper order, who all had unique powers that aided them in their sinister deeds.

They set houses aflame with people in it, executed women and children, killed their livestock, and stole goods, doing anything to get their point across. Many I know, once these invaders came upon their land, wished they'd never been born to just have it all end this way, to have their already short life stolen from them. We only have days to live, and then were gone just like the wildflowers that grow in the fields (Psalms 103:15 NLT). People cried out for mercy, and they received none. Whatever sliver of good that was in Jasper, if any at all, was now eradicated.

Breaking his sister Telina's heart, he left a trail of bloodlike bread crumbs in his wake for the heroes of this story to follow.

"Jasper, what will you say when we arrive, and we don't have the power source? Tambada will surely mock you. We will all look like fools in front of everyone," said a man with a black hood covering his face. He then raised one hand up and pointed a finger at his leader. "Maybe someone else should take charge of this mission." An odd color light began to emerge from his hand.

"Enough! We are all on the same side. If it were easy to acquire, then we'd have found it by now, so lay off," said Tresden.

The man just muttered to himself. Jasper watched him storm off as he spoke under his breath, "Soon things will change around here." He was beginning to become more anxious to accept the devious plan that the beast was prudent of while they edged closer to Tambada's kingdom, preparing for a battle that he knew was imminent.

He wanted to kill every man aboard in his sleep to please Raka, prove his loyalty, but arriving to one of his comrades estates alone whom he hated wouldn't be wise.

The notorious men of the evil lord who is feared by countless pressed on while sea creatures of the dark crevices of the planet that lay dormant until their master called upon them, attacking enemy vessels that tried to cease Montorious's henchmen's every inch. Some went to go protect certain borders while other beasts followed them to their destination to aid them in their efforts against the rebel scum while storm clouds began to cluster together in the sky. The sea raged, thrashing violently against the ship, while the saber tigers rushed to get to safety below. A sudden wave hit the ship once more, sweeping two of the cats off into the ocean. Men shouted, rushing to tie things down.

Jasper held on to the rail of the ship while water thrashed incessantly onto the ship's deck. He wiped his face, gazing at one of his shipmates who had his back turned. Jasper squinted his eyes, gripping the railing tighter as he began to hear voices in his ear wishing him to do evil things.

"Kill him. Kill him now."

Jasper slowly made his way to this worm while the wind blew hard, making the rain go sideways, making it slightly hard to see. He slowly pulled out a giant knife from his satchel on his hip. Finally to his target, he raised the blade high in the air, ready to pierce him in the back, shattering his bones.

Lightning struck suddenly, shooting down, catching a rope on fire. This made the mysterious man turn around. "Jasper!? What the hell are you doing!?" asked the man in the green hood.

"Goodbye" said Jasper.

Before he could make contact, the man shot out a blue orb from his hand, pushing his attacker back.

"You're a fool. You dare betray us?" He then pulled out his sword, charging his assailant on the wet deck where giant puddles had formed everywhere.

"I'm sick of all of you! I deserve more power! And for that to happen, you all must die!"

The two then struggled to get the upper hand, falling onto the slippery deck, wrestling like animals.

"Montorious will have your head for this, you bastard!"

"That may be true, but first, I will have yours!" Jasper punched him in the face relentlessly, in which the man became disarrayed, trying to reach for his weapon, but his enemy now wielded it. "Wait, wait," he pleaded.

Jasper stood over him, his dark damp hair covering his face partially, dripping water. He breathed heavily.

The voices then came back. "Do it, do it!"

He grinned wide, raising the sword high, bringing it down through his old comrade's mouth. Blood poured on the deck. He quickly removed the sword and dragged his body to the edge of the ship and tossed him overboard along with his weapon. "Good riddance."

The blood that had poured from his body was quickly washed away from the deck by the heavy rain. He didn't worry of what the others would say since he'd just tell him that the storm swept him away doing their routine deck jobs.

Do not have pity for him. He was an evil man, deserving the end he received. Darker times are at hand. The enemy kills their own for greed and lust for power. More will be unveiled in this story…of the true enemy of this world.

It was now the next morning, and the sea had returned to its calm state. The men were eating breakfast just a few hours away from their destination. One of the men tossed a plate of meat onto the deck. The big cats fought over who'd get the biggest share.

"It's been thirty minutes, where's Kelgar?" asked one of the mates.

Jasper had his feet propped up. "He had an unfortunate accident. The sea had claimed him."

Everyone became silent. The look in their eyes said enough. Though there was no proof of foul play, sometimes things are better left unsaid. But the only thing that ran through these men's mind was "Who's next?"

CHAPTER 7

Scar Gains Supernatural Powers

Scar held the crystal in his hand, sitting at a table on the top deck alone, observing it in his hand while surges of light radiated. He wanted to crush the power crystal into his hand that very moment, but fear stopped him. What would he become? Was it possible that he'd become something far worse than Montorious? Many things clouded his judgment. He began to think tossing it into the sea was best, but no. Then someone else would discover it, of course. He knew it had to be him to make this sacrifice, one that could change the outcome of this war.

Adam was also going to endure this endeavor with him. The third crystal still hadn't been found. However, it was awaiting its true master to claim it. They were just one day and six hours from their destination, and anticipation rose within the crew. They had strong hopes that the power sources would be a great success.

The farther the ship went into unknown territory, the more sea creatures they encountered. Scar sensed he was getting closer to something evil. It wasn't Jasper or Tambada, no. Someone was playing a dangerous game. Betrayal was afoot yet again. If he found out who it was, they would pay dearly. Too many lives had already been lost, oh, but how easily is the weak mind of man corrupted, being pawns of a war for dark forces we could not fathom.

Many other nations decided to join the most feared, mightiest tyrant on Vospheron. Others were made into slaves and were sent to work for Akachi. Why does it matter where they went? As if they're leaders in their regions didn't already treat them as cattle to be put up for slaughter.

Scar began to think about all the friends he'd lost for freedom. His heart felt empty. He couldn't believe Kanos and his brothers were gone. Flashes of his last memory of them raced like moving pictures in his mind. He began to tremble, closing his eyes. "No, no," said Scar.

"You shall fail, boy. Did I not tell you this long ago? But also, isn't a day like a thousand years and a thousand years as a day? You're weak. You've deceived yourself in thinking you have to fight. The world was already doomed long before this. Just let history play out, Scar, and join me. Together we can defeat Montorious! You know this is the only way," said a mysterious voice he knew too well.

For the first time, he didn't disagree with the vile ghost. Instead, his own mind began to turn on him.

"Maybe I should? No, no, I'm a fool. What's become of me?" he asked himself aloud.

The evil spirit Raka laughed maniacally. "No one shall blame you. You will be the hero once again."

Before Scar could reply, someone put a hand on his shoulder, which startled him, making him drop the crystal on to the ground of the deck. He spun around, sweating. It was only Adam. "Are you all right, my friend? Something is troubling you deeply, no? I've seen that look in many painful eyes."

Scar picked up the crystal, placing it back into a small bag, and tied it then placed it back into his pocket. He then sighed deeply. "I've had dark thoughts…of joining the dark side from…the ghost I told you about."

Adam nodded his head, discerning. "You know, he sounds like a great deceiver, and remember that the evil one comes in many ways, but he will soon be crushed and thrown into the abyss. And we will eradicate this planet from all the enemies who threaten it. Sure as heck won't be easy though." Adam grinned. "But together, brother, we will persevere."

Scar looked at his friend, observing the strong confidence in his eyes, then took a deep breath and exhaled and nodded. "Then let's do some training like the old days back on the island."

Adam grinned once more. "Yeah, when I always kicked your ass."

The two laughed, reminding each other of old stories as they made their way belowdecks to train for their next mission. Scar had gained his confidence back that day but almost lost his soul.

The two trained all day and night, fierce training, for it was only hours away now that they'd be at Tambada's rumored whereabouts. Men were eager to fight as they wanted revenge, though it'll surely be their downfall.

Soldiers shouted up on the top deck, "Look! There it is!"

There was a tiny speck in the distance.

"Quiet, you imbecile!" said Ezra. "You must want them to know we're coming?"

"I'm sure they've already taken wind," replied a soldier.

The closer they approached, the more massive the castle looked.

Scar and Adam rushed to the top deck. "It's just as big as Zepa's fortress was."

Suddenly, dozens of arrows that were aflame soared in the air toward them and rained down out of the sky. The man steering the ship was struck with an arrow for he decided to peep his head out to get a closer look. He instantly died.

The ship crashed into the rocks near the shore as men screamed, being struck by arrows. They fell over to the side to their deaths as others jumped off and ran to the enemy. Other barbarians accompanied Scar and quickly jumped off by the hundreds, confronting giant beasts with massive clubs. It was a massacre.

"We're all going to die," said Ezra, who covered his face in despair.

Suddenly, arrows stopped raining down on them. Men still jumped off the ship while many had already made it to the castle, fighting on the ledges that surrounded it. As the ramp of their ship was finally let down connecting to the shore, Adam and Scar exchanged looks, knowing it was time. The two pulled out their crystals that surged off immense light, then both picked up rocks and placed the gems on the ledge, smashing the crystals then embracing the power source that combined with them. It rained down like snow of many colors around the two as it shone even brighter.

Hideous creatures stormed up the ramp to slaughter them as everyone else was down below fighting. But everyone was then blinded by the light.

So it had begun. The two finally opened the crystals, but now they were forced to keep whatever gift it had given them as they must face hundreds of men and monsters alone. Will they be captured, or will this new power give them what they prayed would be their survival?

CHAPTER 8

The Fall of Tambada

THE LIGHT THAT SHONE OFF THE TWO men began to fade. One was the color turquoise and the other white with an intricate pink design embedded in it. Carnivorous beasts that stood by waiting for the right moment to attack now saw the light leave from the two men, who still looked the same. Nothing had changed. They all began to laugh, mocking them harshly as the men who accompanied them did as well, taunting them.

"Will you two hold hands as you perish slowly?" one asked.

"I'm going to tear off your limbs one by one!" another shouted.

The two heroes' minds raced with confusion. Why didn't the crystals work? They could hear their fellow comrades crying out for mercy as some were ripped in half, eaten, set on fire, shot, and thrown off buildings. Regardless of this shocking outcome, they ran down the ramp yelling, facing the hundreds of monsters and men alone, slicing off heads and limbs. Breaking through wave after wave, the two very skilled brothers in arms did tremendous work, but for how long? Can the heroes of this tail survive such a mass of the enemy's affliction?

They pressed on deeper, almost to the heart of Tambada's kingdom, while there was still no sign of him. Adam knew he'd show his face eventually, then he would finally finish this accursed rival between them once and for all.

The men saw how Scar and Adam continued to show power and courage despite the failed crystals. This too gave them hope, and they began to fight harder, pushing through the enemy's forces as a few new creatures appeared—sludge monsters, massive hounds, beasts that had dozens of eyes. Some were covered in spikes and had tails that were on fire.

"Hey, Scar! We should split up!" said Adam.

"You're right, we can cover more ground that way," replied Scar.

The two then ran off in separate directions, facing obstacles of many sorts along the way as of course, the vile enemy had traps laid throughout, the devious cretins.

"They're getting closer. Shall I call forth your exit?" asked a man to an unknown person who was sitting in a chair, looking out onto the city.

"Haha. No, you fool! Why would I flee? Do you dare think that I believe I'm no match for thee?" Before the man could reply, the man in the chair stood up and threw a dagger at his head, killing him. "Let that be a lesson for the rest of you. You choose your words more wisely."

Jasper, who was in the far corner, snickered.

"They shall never reach this far. Scar is vastly outnumbered," said Tambada.

Scar continued to prove his enemy wrong, edging closer to the center of the city as more drastic actions were taken from Tambada, who sent forth battalions to cease their coming while the enemy had already surrounded Scar from everywhere, appearing on rooftops and coming out of buildings. The battalion of men marched to him in two lines, blocking his path.

"Your advancement ends here!" said the man in front of his brigade.

Scar's armor was stained with blood. *Damn*, he spoke in his mind as it raced, trying to help him think of a way to get out of this one as one man yelled and charged him. Scar let out one hand, making a gesture, taunting him, but instead, something shot out at lightning speed. The man was sliced in half as the odd-shaped weapon then hit another man that made him look like cow meat. The many enemy forces that surrounded him who thought they had him on the ropes were now silent. The only thing you could hear was fighting elsewhere.

Scar's eyes grew wide as he examined his hand, then at the pile of flesh that use to be a man. *The crystal finally revealed its power to me. I wonder what else I can do?* he said in his mind as he began to grin wide. "You guys are in trouble now." Scar raised his hands, aiming them at the men on the ledges as oddly shaped objects shot out his hand, killing them. The men below charged him all at once, raising their shields in defense. Surely now our friend would be captured.

But all of a sudden, his eyes began to grow hazy. Scar thought he'd been hit with a sleeping dart from behind. He yelled, dropping his sword while he heard his enemy closing in. He rose back up, opening his eyes fully as immense light beamed out, blue and purple light that shot out to his foes. He did a 360 and hit the ones behind him as well. This made them all freeze immediately and turn into stone in their wake.

Scar's forehead dripped sweat immensely as his eyes shifted across the destruction he'd created. He grinned wide, then ran off deeper into the city with his newfound powers. He now knew that he had a few more surprises in store, now wreaking his own havoc.

Tambada watched as his city became engulfed by the enemy. Oh, how it fed his soul to see them die. He was searching for his old nemesis, feeling enticed for he knew he'd be here soon to try and slay him. He began to prepare for the battle ahead, putting on his fancy armor, swords, and other garments.

"Sire!" shouted a beast who'd just swooped in on a flying creature who had a few arrows on its hide.

"What is it?"

"It's Scar. He has these…powers now." The monster trembled.

"Don't be a worm!" his leader shouted. He then shot a large orb at him, which made him clench his chest. He was then pierced with a sword. "There is no room for cowards such as this in my ranks." Tambada then removed the sword that dripped goo as the decrepit body fell onto the ground. "Scar must've used one of the crystals on himself. That bastard succeeded in wielding its power for his own."

He gritted his teeth as the many blue saber tigers that surrounded his palace ran out of the room, all suddenly roaring.

Adam was just below, breaching the front gate.

Tambada looked below as he had twelve men with him. "So it begins again." He grinned wide. "Come, come, Adam!"

He could hear loud banging coming from below, then a loud crash.

They breached inside. Adam fought his way to the top as his men stayed below. Saber tigers roared, attacking recklessly. Some had fallen to their deaths as they tried to pounce on him as he continued to dive out of the way and slice some in two, making his way to the main door, which was already open. His enemy was nowhere in sight.

He closed the massive doors and barricaded the exit, then proceeded farther into the sanctum. "Show yourself! Are you afraid to face me after all this time?"

A sinister laugh erupted, and out of the darkness stepped Tambada from the far other side of the room. "You know you can't beat me. You're but a mere human, and my powers have grown since our last encounter. So I give you one last chance to surrender and kneel." Tambada glared at Adam, awaiting his reply.

Adam stared at him for a moment, gripping his sword. "I've already made my choice. Now face me so we can end this charade!"

Tambada's eyes began to glow. "So be it!" He then raised both his hands. The one that was robotic still channeled energy out of it thanks to Xsuss's advanced technology after that bastard Adam sliced it off back on Fee'unn.

While his hands were in the air, the entire room began to shake. Giant orbs began to shoot out his hands and just float to the ceiling as some engulfed below as well.

One brushed Adam's shoulder, giving him a deep shock. He clenched up a bit. "So is this your game? Having little tricks to defeat me?" Adam then charged him, dodging the orbs as best as he could, but kept hitting them as he approached his enemy. Almost upon Tambada, he yelled, jumping into the air.

Tambada pulled out two swords and deflected his attack as the two began their personal vendetta once more, yelling and shouting cruel things to one another while the orbs slowly began to dissipate after a while. Giving Adam leverage, though the room was being decimated by their battle, more saber tigers tried to breach inside to assist their leader. He was getting the upper hand, and he managed to kick Adam in his gut with a martial arts move. Adam coughed up blood, then Tambada swung a mighty punch to his face that made him fall to the ground, dropping his weapon. His enemy then kicked it away from him, then dragged his body to the ledge to throw him over.

"Oh, I do pity we come to the end with our time together." Tambada pierced Adam in his shoulder with his sword.

Adam cried out in agony, and his enemy raised his sword to remove his head. All of a sudden, Adam began to yell again, clutching his stomach.

"Oh, I didn't hit you that hard, boy, get over it! You'll soon be dead anyway and see your family again."

Adam then kicked Tambada in his leg as hard as he could. This made him back up for a moment. Adam was now rolling on the ground, digging his nails deeply into the cement, leaving claw marks. His hair began to fall out of his head, and his yells became more of a terrifying roar.

Tambada watched this play out in confusion and somewhat fear. "What sorcery is this?" he asked aloud to himself.

Adam's armor burst off his body, flying up in the air. His pants ripped while his legs expanded and became massive with fur, while the rest of his body began to grow rapidly and with fur as well.

Tambada created massive energy balls and hit them all over Adam's body, but there wasn't any effect.

Adam now stood up on his two giant feet. He'd become something else covered in red and white fur. He spun his head around, growling and dripping spit that sizzled once it touched something for it was acid. His eyes were bright blue with a black slit in the middle.

Tambada charged him and sliced his body up in many places. The beast roared, dripping blood, but his skin began to heal itself.

Tambada backed up as his eyes widened. "So you too have one of the crystals! Out of everyone, it chose you!?"

Adam was losing control, throwing things and hitting walls.

Tambada shouted once more to get the vile brute's attention. The monster charged him, crushing the ground with every step as the room shook. He jumped into the air and pounced on him, grasping his neck and throwing him against the wall. Adam suddenly had a sword pierced deep into his side.

"Let go of me, you mongrel!" Tambada raised one hand, punching him in the face and shooting orbs in it that singed his face, but the beast grabbed it and snapped it back. He hollered in agony.

Adam then bit into his neck, ripping off flesh, then carried him over to the ledge, holding him over. Tambada was barely able to keep his eyes open. "How…how does it end like this? I shall not beg for your mercy." He spat into its face.

The beast then roared immensely, then dropped him. At that very moment, the saber tigers burst into the room by the dozens, all pouncing on him at once. He threw many off over the ledge, then took a few steps back into the destroyed chamber. He was slammed against the wall as they sank their thick teeth and claws deep into his flesh. He still roared, spitting out acid as he grabbed some and tore them in two and broke a few of their necks as his body tried to heal itself. However, he was not fast enough from all the repeated attacks. He continued handling them on his own.

There was one blue tiger left. It was the largest, but he made short work of it. Adam was now alone in the dark decimated room that reeked of death.

Men stormed up the stairs into the room. "Whoa, what happened here?" one asked.

"What's that thing!" another shouted.

"Where's Adam? Maybe they both fell over," stated a soldier

"Let's get rid of this new abomination while we're here. Damn that Montorious! Fire!" shouted the man.

Arrows, spears, and guns were fired to eliminate this thing.

Adam evaded the current danger by climbing up the wall as chunks of cement fell down from his enormous hands and feet pressing in. He roared angrily as he looked at them.

"Fire again!"

This time many made their target as Adam roared, yanking the giant spears out of his body and bullets were pushed out of his skin, falling onto the ground. He shortly after fell from the ceiling and got up on his knees, roaring and thrashing his head while acid flew into the air from his mouth.

"Watch out!" a man yelled as some acid hit a soldier's battle mask, eating it away quickly. He rushed to take it off.

Adam rose up again, backing up slowly to the ledge, not paying attention as he began to change back while he was in pain. One leg began to shrink as fur fell off him rapidly. His arms then shrank as well.

"What's this?" a soldier asked Adam, who was now almost himself as he roared one last time as his face morphed back. He then looked up at the men, then passed out and fell over the ledge. whizzing past other fallen dead that were slain from the aerial battle to their doom, passing hundreds of levels of the palace that was aflame as the wind hissed. He suddenly began falling faster now, till someone caught him soaring through the air.

Adam slowly opened his eyes as he later was gingerly placed onto a roof. Water was poured on his face. He leaned up, and his eyes shot open, the color of the beast he was previously, then were now normal. He looked up in awe to see his friend floating just a few feet in front of him.

"The crystal worked, my friend." He then showed him the rest of his abilities as Adam stood up.

"Finally hope."

"So how about you, my friend, what can you do?" asked Scar.

Adam looked down at the ground briefly. "I…think I was fighting Tambada, and then something happened to me. I'm at a loss of what happened, but I'm most certain that Tambada is dead."

Scar's eyes became sharp. "Wouldn't that be something to have a party about." Scar smiled. "Can you still fight? I know we're outmatched, but you and I together can finish them off. Are you able to tap back into your power?" asked Scar.

Before Adam could respond, vast giant birds were coming to the city by the hundreds, blinding one by the mere sight of the colors they bore.

"It's their reinforcements," stated Adam, now back on his feet as they drew closer.

Scar was about to attack until they flew past overhead, attacking the enemy. They wore armor all over their bodies. One of them came where the two heroes were. The bird came down hard with massive talons that crushed the ground beneath it, its feathers filled with mesmerizing colors. "Which one of you is Scar?" the creature asked. "I am Rafta."

Scar flew over to the towering beast that slightly bowed.

"We come in peace, and we've come to help the mighty Scar."

CHAPTER 9

The Majestic Birds of Kinolda

WHILE THE THREE SPOKE ON THE BUILDING, the battle was almost at its end for these fierce birds grasped dozens of men and other creatures into their giant talons, dropping them from heights to their doom.

Scar watched briefly as they reminded him of Taguna in a way as he then began to wonder where he was and would he ever see him again.

"If you two would kindly come back with me to my homeland? My king would like to meet you," stated the bird. He then turned around so that they could climb aboard.

Scar chuckled. "I'm good." He then ran and jumped off the ledge and shot into the air.

Adam just rolled his eyes and slightly smiled. "Show-off." He then climbed upon the massive beast.

"Hold on." The bird then took off into the air. "Don't worry, the rest of your friends are on their way as well."

Scar nodded his head to the creature as they both flew next to each other over the vast ocean, flying for a few hours till they reached a massive island that had many tall intricate structures. Baby birds were in colorful trees in their nests as they watched the warriors from their homeland return in a strategic swift line. The troops continued to pass many other outposts of different-colored birds. There were massive statues and more trees as they then landed in an assembly area where dozens of white birds surrounded them that wore gold armor with blue eyes.

All of a sudden, serene music was playing from above, and all the massive creatures began to bow as a reddish and orange bird came soaring in. He appeared like he was on fire but wasn't. He bore turquoise eyes as he swooped down to where the two humans were and looked deep into their eyes

"You must be the one they call Scar? I've heard much about you, endured such ordeals, and yet you still remain who you are. Your roots go strong in good soil. My name is Toshiro, and I will do what I can to help in your fight for we all live in this world and must do our part. I've been in many wars. This is the second time it will be with a threat that seems to be unstoppable, but I assure you, we can and will not let Vospheron fall."

"Second?" Scar made an expression of curiosity, hoping he'd speak more on the matter.

"It was a long time ago, and they're now all…dead." The bird king looked away for a moment, then turned back. "Well now, I hear that you two acquired two of the crystals and both have consumed them, yes?"

The two nodded.

"That was very brave and stupid. It could've killed you both. Everyone always utilizes their power but never fully takes it in the way of this proportion before. But what's done is done. They will be a great asset."

At that moment, Scar heard loud barking. He turned to see Scout, who was running toward him, and knocked him over, licking his face as his tail sparked off light while his master laughed. "Good to see you too, boy."

Ezra and a few others came into the area where the giant birds stood.

Scar stood back up. "This is it?" he asked.

Ezra looked down. "I'm afraid so."

"You may all stay here for as long as you like," said Toshiro.

The same bird that brought them there showed them where they could rest in their beautiful home. Massive houses were built in the trees, and below were crystal clear blue water and waterfalls. The food that was given was divine—fresh fish, shrimp, clams, crab, lobster, and many other pescatarian delights.

Scar continued to enjoy the serene night that was provided for him and his friends after the victory over Tambada. His mind wandered off a bit, pondering what the crystal had given his closest friend that brought his rival to his bitter end?

Adam just stared down at his plate. It seemed he'd lost something important to him. As flashes of the battle cries ran through his mind, he began to see giant teeth and blood. He picked up his spoon to take another bite of his meal when he felt a sudden sharp pain in his body. He yelled in agony, and his hair stood up like a magnetic fusion was in effect. He fell down to his knees as the men around him stood up.

"Scar! Something's happening to Adam!" shouted a soldier.

Adam's eyes changed multiple colors, then dark blue. His arms began to grow enormously.

"He's bewitched by a demon!" a man shouted.

Scar rushed over to his aid. "Adam?" asked Scar as he crept closer while his friend was breathing heavily. He now was covered in fur. Scar was about to lay a hand upon him until…*wham!* He was tossed across the room and hit a wall. A loud roar erupted, shaking the room. The giant birds surrounded Adam while he still continued to grow in size.

"Stop. This is his fight!" shouted Toshiro.

The birds then stepped back.

Scar burst out of the rubble, flying toward the beast and tackling him to the ground. "Calm down, it's me!"

Adam just growled and spat green acid, but Scar swiftly dodged it as it seeped through the floor. Rapidly he punched the beast in his side multiple times and in the face. The giant birds brought huge ropes that they dropped from above, and they began to move on their own, wrapping around the target, electrifying him. Adam was roaring in anger, trying to break free. Scar quickly reached for his device, pressing multiple buttons, and aimed it above his friend's head for a giant cage was instantly built around him. While the electrical ropes continued to shock him, Adam eventually passed out, still in his horrifying form.

The cage had a force field to shield them from the acid if he awoke. Scar watched as he slumbered. "I'm sorry, my friend, this happened to you. We knew the risks."

Toshiro swept down next to Scar.

"Is there a way to reverse it?" Scar asked.

"Once he becomes one with the crystal, it is too late. He must now learn to tame this power that has been gifted to him."

"Gift? This is a curse!" stated Scar.

"The crystals do not make mistakes. It chose to bond with Adam, and it manifested him into a mighty warrior. Have faith, he will be okay. Until then, stay here, continue to regain your strength. You'll be on your way to seek out the last power source soon."

Weeks passed as the men grew restless to press forward and kill more things. Toshiro had war vessels from his allies long ago that were left there for new humans they'd befriended. The giant Kinolda birds set the ships in the water for them and gave them food and supplies. Before they left, Scar also gave Toshiro a medium-sized device that lit up blue when they needed his help.

Adam was already placed aboard as well, still imprisoned in his beast form. Scar feared he'd never change back. As Floyd was upon his shoulder, he stared at the city of Kinolda as they drifted farther away to sea.

"Scar, come quick!" shouted a crew member.

He rushed below. The man pointed to the cage. Adam looked back at him while he was still a monster. "I'm sorry for trying to rip your face off." Adam slightly grinned, showing his sharp fanged teeth.

Scar almost teared up. "I thought you were gone."

"Me too, but when I focus hard enough, I feel my body trying to morph back. It's just a painful process."

The two talked for a bit longer till Scar made the decision. Adam was safe enough to be released for everything seemed well once more, until Adam lifted his head to the ceiling, sniffing the air. He sensed something was coming. Scar rushed to the top deck and stared at the ocean from left to right but saw nothing. It was an odd feeling that felt powerful and sinister. Surely it had to be the last crystal, but why did this one feel different?

Adam finally came up above, shaking the deck. He stood near his friend and began to growl.

"What is it?" asked Scar.

"Look!" said Floyd.

An armada of ships was approaching with black flags that appeared to have many different fearsome designs and symbols on them. The most standard was one with swords through the eyes of a white skull.

Scar and Adam exchanged looks. They were ready for a fight.

CHAPTER 10

Bloody Pirates!

"D ON'T STOP THE SHIP! KEEP GOING! WE'LL go right through them," said Scar as thousands of men aboard the ships yelled, cursing and saying other taunting words, raising their many varieties of weapons.

The ships began to block them in.

"Hold on!" shouted Scar as the vessel collided with another while the rest were still a few clicks out and made a perimeter. Pirates boarded from every direction. A tall broad man came aboard with a slimy creature beside him. "Argh! What do we have here? What is your name boy?" asked the man who stepped closer.

"Scar."

The man raised his eyebrows. "No. The one who stood up against Montorious all those years ago? Well, shit, my apologies. I guess I'd better let you's go on your merry way, huh?"

His crew all laughed.

Adam growled. "Least he put up a fight. Where were you then?"

The man stood in front of Adam's face and squinted his eyes. "Dealing with things far worse than him. We've traveled to far, distant lands from this region on Vospheron."

Scar felt an unusual feeling once more. He glanced down at the man's wrist, which bore a bracelet that had a shiny crystal imbedded in it. It had many intricate colors. *That must be it*, he pondered to himself.

All of a sudden, Adam yelled and fell to his knees.

The pirate leader backed up a bit as he went through his various changes back to human while the pirate lord's pet hissed. "Well, you don't see that every day, do you, boys!?"

His crew laughed again.

"Ah, I like you guys. You'll be a great asset for my current expedition. A little bird told me that there's valuable treasure close around these parts, and you're all going to help with your freakish powers, and so you better get that witchery under control." He glared at Adam.

Scar knew he could take them all on, but he didn't want to endanger his friends. Pragticus and Obek were trying to stay calm as pirate men were taunting them while women corsairs fancied them and checked their persons to see if they had any weapons they wanted to take. In doing so, one groped Obek. "My, my, I like this one. Hey, baby, how 'bout we fool around for a bit later? My two friends would love to join too." She rubbed one of his shoulders and then caressed his face.

"You want me to jab him in his neck?" whispered Floyd.

"No, behave," said Maria, who was standing behind Scar.

"So it's a plan? My name's Ryker, by the way."

They needed that last crystal. Whatever awaited them at their destination, Scar would grab it when the time was right. It seemed the crystal gave the pirate king the power to acquire great riches and a vast formidable army, but he should beware…one's treasure will be where the heart is, according to Matthew 6:21.

Scar spoke of what he found on Ryker's wrist to Ezra. "I will help in anyway," he stated.

The two shook hands.

As night befell them, Scar lay in his bed while conversing with Floyd, who was across the room feasting on a sea creature, ripping through its carcass as guts and other things from its stomach that were still alive fell onto the floor in a squirming pile.

Scout awoke from his sleep and trotted over, sniffing the pile of foul things, and began to quickly snarf down it all. Disgusting, you say? Yes, very much so, but isn't it not with us as well when we know something or someone isn't right for us, but we ignore the signs as if we were to look into a mirror and completely forget how bad we looked? (James 1:22–25).

Don't return back to old habits that you've been freed from as if you were a dog returning to its vomit (Proverbs 26:11 ERV).

"Can you eat that outside? I don't know why you thought that was a good idea, and it stinks." Scar gave Floyd a scowl as he covered his face with his covers, but then quickly emerged and threw a pillow in his friend's direction, who dodged it and flew to the window.

"Oh, hush, I just wanted a little midnight snack."

Scar shook his head, then tried to get some rest while the ocean waves thrashed all night, swaying the vessels. Ryker wanted to leave early. His men were rushing their ships to be mobilized and turned about.

"Hurry up, you sea rats!" shouted a commander.

The ships were finally off; the wind was fierce. "Yes! We should be there in no time." The pirate lord grinned wide for he couldn't wait to grasp the largest treasure load ever, all thanks to his special map upon his wrist that was like a magnet.

A massive cave was up ahead with a pier. Everyone tied off around the massive giant rocky terrain island with slight vegetation and let down their ramps. Hundreds of thousands of men and a few women in the ranks poured off every ship.

"All right, fan out, I want every piece of gold you can find. Beware the tales of those who dwell in the cavern. They won't be welcoming," said the pirate leader.

"Yes, Lord Ryker!" they all shouted as they bore all varieties of weapons and other garments being from different countries from all parts of the world.

Scar followed the king into the cave with his friends. "You know you can stay behind if you're not up for this." Scar looked at Maria, teasing, as she rolled her eyes.

"What would you do without my expertise? Be lost without me." She looked deep into his eyes, then walked past him up ahead.

Scar wasn't paying attention and ran into a wall. Floyd pecked his head. "The beasts of the night won't need to take us out. You're doing just fine on your own."

"Oh, be quiet you." Scar raised his hand into a fist to his friend's face.

Floyd just chuckled.

Up ahead were six tunnels. Everyone dispersed. They walked for thirty minutes, and the entire time, there were giant bugs that scurried beneath and above them that they burned with their torches.

"There isn't anything here. I think the boss's coordinates were off."

"He relies on that crystal too much, it's drained his mind," said his crewmates who were way ahead.

"Shut your mouth. Do you think this would be easy to find in here?" said another while another grew tired and decided to rest against the wall.

All of a sudden, there was mass yelling and guns blazing that echoed. The halls rang with torment into your ears.

"What's going on!" Ryker was smoking a cigar as he rushed up ahead and saw men on the ground dead and a wall close back up. There was a sudden loud howl, and Scar looked beside him.

"It wasn't me." Adam grinned.

"Think this is funny? My men are dying!" Ryker grabbed him by his shirt, then pushed him. "Keep moving!" he shouted as more of his men rushed ahead.

This time there was a loud squawk as a giant bird man swooped down with two swords and sliced the heads off two pirates. "Leave this place!" it shouted.

CHAPTER 11

Battle with the Guardians

"FOLLOW THAT THING!" SHOUTED RYKER, CURSING AS everyone chased this new weird creature through the tunnel. It brought them to a massive spot where all the pirates were led, fighting these beast men. There was a bear with wings, an ape that was using a staff, pulverizing every pirate that attacked him, a wolf that had gray and blue fur that stood on its hind legs with a long snout that held a spear and a sword on his waist. He pointed his spear at them.

"Up there!"

Something was crawling up the wall to them that had long white hair that appeared to move by itself, lashing out and grasping the pirate leader, throwing him across the room.

"We must save him!" shouted a pirate."

"No, he'd want us to gather the gold first!" said another.

"We will," said Scar as he Ezra, Adam, Maria, Pragticus, and Obek slid down the steep cliff. As they jumped over some unconscious but mostly dead men, they were stopped by a beast that had four arms. Above it looked reptilian, and below it was yellow covered in spikes. It had purple eyes and a scorpion tail.

"I'll handle this!" Adam yelled as he fell to his knees.

The man creature just laughed. "Is he sick?"

"Are you sure you can control it?" asked Scar.

"Go!" Adam raised his head. His eyes had already changed color and was growing in size.

The creature stopped smiling. "Well, well. It can't be."

"Hurry, now's our chance," said Ezra.

Adam was only halfway in his form, but stood up and charged him anyway while Ezra was already on his way to Ryker, who was unconscious. He ran then slid to him on his knees, frantically searching for the bracelet.

Scar was beside him now. "You have the honor in keeping the last one."

He stood up, examining it as he yanked it out of what it was held in, now grinning at Scar. "Oh, I do love what's about to happen next."

Scar made a confused expression.

A loud growl was then heard behind him. He spun around, and the wolf beast pounced on him.

"You're not getting through. He can't be—"

Before he could finish his sentence, Maria hit him over the head with a massive rock.

Scar looked up at her and scowled. "He was telling me something important." He then turned to see Ezra rushing down to another tunnel. "No!" he shouted, about to take off into the air, staring at Ezra, who was getting away.

"Next time, I'll let him eat you." Maria had her arms crossed.

Scar just grabbed her arm and took off into the air. She screamed as they soared off to where Ezra went off to while the pirates kept these mystic beings at bay by their sheer numbers.

"Hey, what about us!" shouted Pragticus, who was still with Obek, but the two then suddenly were face-to-face with a massive creature that had purple fur and orange eyes. It was growling and looking down at them, drooling from its mouth. It was on top of the ceiling.

Drool fell on Pragticus's head. "Ah, of all the things!"

Obek laughed as they both then lifted their heads to the ceiling to see what awaited them. "Well, this is just great. How many of you are there?" asked Obek.

The monster just roared, then spoke, "We won't let you release him." It then dropped from above, pouncing its enormous body on the two heroes.

Scar continued to soar in the air, holding Maria, as they passed many deactivated traps and another area that had been opened from the button on the wall to the right. Scar came back to the ground, setting his friend down. As they crept inside, there were hieroglyphics all over the walls and a big hole, a pit. Ezra stood whispering something.

"Ezra, what're you doing? How did you know this was here?"

He looked back at Scar with an evil grin, and his face was hideous and distorted.

Maria pulled out a gun and shot at him multiple times all over his body.

CHAPTER 12

The Wariu Hito Arrives

SCAR TOOK OFF WITH IMMENSE SPEED, SHOOTING off blue and purple lasers from his eyes, but Ezra only raised his hand, deflecting them. He then grasped Scar's neck and let out a sinister growl, then whispered in his ear, "It's time to show you who I really am." He then flung Scar across the room.

Scar hit the wall hard as rubble fell on him. Maria cursed and rushed over to him with Floyd hovering over him. Scar slowly got up.

"Why do you always pick the bad guys for allies?"

"Shut up, Floyd. I didn't know." He spat out blood.

"Now, enough meddling!" Ezra chanted the rest of his ancient words, then flew over the pit that began to close. You could hear sudden terrible screams coming from it and gnashing of teeth. He placed the crystal into the wall, and the entire wall began to glow the same colors of the power source, then exploded with a dark, eerie aura. Then mist came as the crystal floated in the air.

"Um, Scar, I think it's time to leave," said Maria as she grasped her friend's hand.

"Right." He was about to take off into the air until he spotted a ghoulish hand reach out and grasp the power source from out of the mist. Evil laughter commenced. His heart dropped. "You guys hang on to me!" Scar took off as fast as he could.

He could hear Ezra shout, "That's right, run!" He dared not look back for he knew what his devious companion had done. He had released what would truly bring hell on Vospheron.

Ghouls poured out of the mist, swarming the room, descending to the ground, awaiting their leader. A six-foot-nine ghoulish being walked out of the mist with a teenage boy by his side and the crystal in the other hand. He then crushed it as the power surged through his veins, savoring it. He tilted his head back for a moment, closing his eyes, inhaling the fresh air, then tilted his head back up with his eyes slowly opening. He exhaled. "Finally, I've claimed back what was taken from me!" His eyes shone red. He threw his hands into the air as they slowly became a little more human. "Now is the time, old friends. We take this world back for our own!"

Tens of thousands were in the surrounding area as millions were behind in the other creepy other unworldly world, still waiting to come out. Many dragons hovered in the sky, their bones showing in many parts of their massive bodies as skin was slowly reforming tissue. They were waiting as well.

"All hail Raka!" many shouted.

Ezra knelt in front of him, but Raka scoffed. "Rise." He placed a hand on his shoulder, looking deep into his eyes. "You did well… little brother."

About the Author

Frederick Alexander is of the Christian faith who graduated from Jamestown High School and loves to cook many different ethnic foods. His inspiration for writing the book was he wanted to create a different world no one ever thought of. With God's help, many more stories are to be told with hidden messages to all who will heed them.